More Praise for *Heart's Delight*

"Passionate, romantic. . . ." —*KLIATT*

"Readers who want to experience a romance from a male point of view will find it appealing." —*SLJ*

"Nilsson effectively creates a hero of raw vulnerability . . . there's a sympathy and a perception in the depiction of the boy's naiveté . . . and his affection and pain." —*The Bulletin*

1999 Dutch "Silver Kiss"

1997 Deutscher Jugendliteraturpreis

1992 First prize in Rabén & Sjögren's awards competition for best love story

heart's delight

heart's delight

PER NILSSON

TRANSLATED BY TARA CHACE

Simon Pulse

New York London Toronto Sydney

ᵂᴹ

SIMON PULSE
An imprint of Simon & Schuster Children's Publishing Division
1230 Avenue of the Americas, New York, NY 10020
Text copyright © 1992 by Per Nilsson
English translation copyright © 2003 by Tara Chace
First published in the United States by Front Street, 2003
This translation was produced with the support of the Svenska Institute of Stockholm, Sweden
Originally published in Sweden by Rabén & Sjögren Bokforlag under the title *Hjärtans Fröjd*
All rights reserved, including the right of reproduction in whole or in part in any form.
SIMON PULSE and colophon are registered trademarks of Simon & Schuster, Inc.
Manufactured in the United States of America
First Simon Pulse edition June 2005
10 9 8 7 6 5 4 3 2 1
The Library of Congress has cataloged the hardcover edition as follows:
Nilsson, Per
[Hjärtans Fröjd. English.]
Heart's delight / Per Nilsson; translated by Tara Chace.—1st U.S. ed.
p. cm.
Summary: As a sixteen-year-old looks at and systematically destroys each of his mementos of Ann-Katrin, he replays scenes from their relationship and realizes that it was not the great romance he believed it to be.
ISBN 1-886910-92-8 (alk. paper) (hc.)
[1. Love—Fiction. 2. Coming of age—Fiction. 3. Sweden—Fiction.]
I. Chace, Tara. II. Title.
PZ7.N5888Kj 2003
[Fic]—dc21   2003051167
ISBN 0-689-87677-7 (pbk.)

Contents

heart's delight

The building is a very normal Swedish apartment building with three stories and four main entrances.

The building is called "7" and the entrances are called A, B, C, and D. It's in the suburbs of a city in Sweden. Around it are other, similar buildings. A little farther away, on the other side of the square, there are taller buildings.

Now, if you for some reason had been standing outside the A entrance that Saturday night between nine p.m. and one a.m., what would you have seen and heard?

1. No one left the building through entrance A.
2. No one entered the building through entrance A.
3. Off a balcony on the second floor, someone threw
   a. a potted plant
   b. a big black frisbee
   c. a Swiss army knife
4. From the same balcony, someone released
   d. five light-colored oblong balloons
5. The light was still on in only one apartment (on the second floor) at one a.m.

And if you had gone into stairwell A, what would you have seen and heard during the same period of time?

1. Someone used the garbage chute several times.
2. Someone went down to the basement with a sheet and then came up again, right away, without the sheet.
3. Someone from an apartment on the second floor went up and rang the doorbell to an apartment on the third floor but ran away before the door opened.

That's what you would have seen and heard.

That's all that happened.

Well, actually, one more thing!
    At exactly one a.m. . . .

Third-person sing., masc.

A boy, or a young man, is sitting alone in his room in an apartment on the second floor of a three-story building. It's a Saturday night in August. There's a full moon.

He lied so he could be home alone on this night. He lied to his mom. He said, "No, I'm staying home this weekend. I'm not coming. I'm supposed to meet Henke. We're going to a club . . . a new dance club that's opening."

It wasn't true.

He hadn't talked to Henke since school got out. He just wanted to be alone on this night. He needed to be alone. It was absolutely necessary that he be alone on this Saturday night, the last Saturday night of the summer.

And his mom believed him and left for the cabin with Krister and Hanna:

"See you Sunday . . ."

Maybe, he thought.

Now the boy, or the young man, is sitting at his desk and gathering a bunch of things together. It looks like he's organizing the things or sorting them.

When he's done, he leans back and looks at the clock. Five to nine. He nods to himself and lets his eyes wander over the items collected on his desk. From left to right he's lined up in a row:

a bus pass
a postcard
a German grammar book
a potted plant
a packet of seeds
a page from a songbook
a record
an empty plastic box
a package of condoms
a wadded-up sheet
a frayed American flag
a black notebook
a wrapped package with a curly ribbon
a movie ticket
a razor blade and a bottle of blue pills.

Everything must go, he thinks.

On the bookshelf to the right of the desk is a phone. He gives it an almost imperceptible glance before he turns his eyes back toward the window.

It's starting to get dark out there and he can see his face reflected in the glass. As still as a statue, he sits and contemplates the reflection of a pale and serious boy, or young man.

A boy or a young man?

What should I call him?

He lives with his mom and his pretend dad, Krister, he has a roof over his head, he gets food every day and clothes when he needs them. And a little money. He goes to school. He doesn't need to be responsible or worry. He doesn't need to shave. He's probably a boy.

But:

He has a voice like a man and hair on his body. (Not on his chest, no.) He's tall like a grownup. He knows just as much as most grownups do. And more than some. He should be able to handle things.

And he has loved.

He might be a man. A young man.

What should I call him?

I'll call him: He.

Third-person singular, masculine:

He.

Before Heart's Delight

Before Heart's Delight, I was a boy, he thinks.

Before Heart's Delight, I was a child.

I was a sensible child who believed that there were sensible explanations for everything, he thinks.

And I believed that there are certain people who understand how everything fits together, who see everything clearly, who can stand a little bit outside of things and see through everything, he thinks. That there are some people who don't allow themselves to be fooled, who . . . who are in control, who . . . I thought I was that kind of person, he thinks.

But that was before Heart's Delight.

Now he looks at the clock again. He sees that it's nine o'clock now. It's time to begin.

He takes a deep breath.

Now. Now the show can begin. The final show.

HEART'S DELIGHT
Screenplay & Direction: He himself

(Or perhaps she . . . , he thinks.)
    In the leading role: He himself
(Or perhaps she . . . , he thinks.)
    For audiences age 15 and over

Will there be ads before the movie?
No, no ads before *Heart's Delight*.

A bus pass

All the way on the left, first in the long row of objects on his desk, is a bus pass.

He picks it up, holds it in front of himself, stares at it: a normal bus pass.

If you live more than three miles from school you get a bus pass. And since all the high schools are in the city and almost all the people live outside the city, almost everyone needs a bus pass to get to school.

If you lose your bus pass, you can pay fifty Swedish crowns and get a new one. If you lose that one too, you have to pay six hundred crowns.

He hadn't lost his a single time.

He'd had it in his wallet from the time school started in August almost exactly a year ago until school got out in June. Every school day he'd ridden the bus for thirty-five minutes to get to school and forty minutes to get home from school. Changing at Marketplace.

The first few weeks in the fall, the bus rides had been infinitely long and tiresome, then he'd gotten used to them, and then, then there was a time during spring semester when he felt like the bus rides were entirely too short and went by way too fast, a time when he would gladly have ridden the bus for several hours to get to school.

Yes. That's how it was.

It had started on the bus.

He sighs and tears the bus pass into two pieces. And then into four pieces. And into eight pieces. Sixteen. Thirty-two. When the bus pass is just sixty-four very small bits of yellow paper, he gathers them up in his palm and goes to the bathroom, to the toilet.

After he flushes, he sees that a single little bit of paper jumped up onto the inside of the toilet bowl to escape its death by drowning. He pokes it down with the toilet brush and flushes again.

So there, yes, he thinks, and he's about to go back to his room when he sees that the bit of yellow paper survived this time too and is lying there, floating around in circles in the water.

He mutters something to himself as he bends and picks up the little scrap of paper. Then he rolls it into a very small, moist yellow ball, goes out of the apartment, out into the stairwell, down to the garbage chute. He opens it and flicks the little ball of paper with his index finger off his thumb down into the garbage chute.

"There."

Who would have thought it would be so hard to kill a bus pass, he thinks as he goes back into the apartment.

Back to his room and back to his desk. On the bookshelf, the phone sits silently.

Heart's Delight on the bus

She came in from the fog
Her red hair
Lit up my morning
Lit up my life

That's what he'd written in his black book, but was it true? Was it really foggy that morning?

Had he really seen her red hair even as the bus slowed down, pulling up to the stop?

Could he even remember the first time? He might have seen her on the bus several times before without noticing her. Maybe she'd been taking the bus all fall, ever since school started?

The movie-theater-in-his-head had played all the scenes of this movie so many times now that he no longer knew which ones were actual memories.

And now the final show had begun, and then the movie would never be shown again.

This is the way it was, he decides. This is how it had been:

One foggy morning in November he was sitting as

usual in the very back of the bus on his way to school.

As the bus slowly pulled up to the stop he noticed something red, something red that wasn't usually there, and when the redheaded girl with the moss-green cotton jacket got on, he thought she lit up the whole bus.

Yes, that's how it had been the first time he saw her. Did he know even then that she was Heart's Delight?

Maybe he knew it. At any rate, he sat and watched for the whole bus ride in order to catch a glimpse of her standing up at the front of the packed bus, and when he hopped off at Marketplace he rushed up alongside the bus to catch a glimpse of her from outside the bus before it drove on.

From that morning on, he was filled with longing. A longing he had never felt before, one that didn't have any other goal than that she, the girl with the red hair, would be on the bus as he rode to school.

Soon he discovered that she took the same bus he did every Monday, Tuesday, and Thursday morning.

On the way home from school he never saw her. He didn't know where she went, he didn't know what she did during the day, he didn't know who she was, what her name was, where she lived. He knew only that she filled him with longing.

The weekends were suddenly way too long now.

Wednesdays and Fridays were bad.

Mondays, Tuesdays, and Thursdays were good, of course, but not good enough. He wanted to see her more. He wanted to see her better.

So now he started his slow journey-toward-the-front-of-the-bus. While the wintry weeks went by, he advanced slowly forward from his seat way in the back, one seat a week.

By the middle of February he had made it all the way up so that he was sitting diagonally across from the driver, in the seat closest to the aisle, and sometimes the girl with the red hair stood right next to him, so close that her leg brushed against his when the bus lurched going around a turn. But that still wasn't good, because now he was sitting so close that he didn't dare look at her.

So he started his slow journey-toward-the-back-of-the-bus. By the end of March he had reached the perfect place: far enough away to be able to study her without her noticing and close enough to see her brown eyes.

Red hair, brown eyes, and moss-green jacket.

The flag of his dream country was red, brown, and green.

And every Monday, Tuesday, and Thursday she was really there and lit up his morning and his life.

And then came a Wednesday:

There was no English class the first two periods that

day and he didn't go to school until nine-thirty.

The bus was almost empty.

He was so unprepared—it was Wednesday, after all—that he didn't discover her until she was already on the bus and heading straight for him.

Dear God, if you're out there, let her sit next to me, he thought. Dear God, let her . . . no, wait, no, I changed my mind, no, not next to me, no no . . .

She sat in front of him across the aisle.

He exhaled and started staring at her hair, the back of her neck, her ear. Just a few inches away from him. Her ear. His heart was filled with . . . tenderness. Almost with sadness. Her ear looked so vulnerable, little and lonely with small, soft folds. The neck and back belonged to a proud young woman, but the ear was a little girl's.

He sat there and just stared at her ear until suddenly she stood up and got off at a stop.

He looked around in confusion. He had missed Marketplace, he'd gone through half the city, he would be a half-hour late for math and Mr. Knutsson would glare at him and give him two extra pages of homework.

But it was worth it.

Before he got off he noticed this: a faint scent of lemon still lingered in the empty bus.

A postcard

He picks up a pale yellow postcard off his desk. On the front of the postcard there's a picture of a cat's head and one of a girl with a catlike face, and a little text under the two pictures:

"The CAT, by nature, is soft, flexible, coquettish, and false; with its soft, silky paws it invites caresses, but pays the caressing hand back by scratching it."
—*Loosely from Sophus Schack's Studies in Physiognomy, 1880*

On the back of the postcard, written quickly and carelessly, it says:

Saw this card.
Made me think of you.
Can you think why?
                    Björn

And her name and address.
    The stamp was postmarked in Gothenburg.

He takes a lighter out of his desk drawer, sets fire to one corner of the postcard, lets it burn and char, and doesn't drop it until the flames start to lick at his fingers.

"Ouch!"

He gathers up the ash that's left after the card has burned up and blows it out the window.

"It smells like burning cat," he mumbles to himself, opening the window a little more. "It smells like burned cat."

The telephone sits silently on the bookshelf.

Heart's Delight gets a name

If only the word "if" hadn't existed . . .

Would everything still have happened, only some other way? Or would it not have happened at all?

If only he and Henke hadn't sat across from each other on the bus on the way home from school one day in April.

If only she hadn't happened to be on the same bus for the first time ever on her way home from the city.

If only she hadn't happened to sit in front of them on the bus, close enough to hear them.

If only Henke hadn't started talking about his favorite thing: comic books.

If only Henke hadn't said that Spider-Man was the greatest and most interesting comic-book hero of all time.

If only he hadn't teased Henke:

"Spider-Man, ugh, that gross insect. Duh, the greatest comic-book hero in world history isn't a spider, it's a duck, everyone knows that."

"What?" gasped Henke, pretending to be irritated.

"A duck, DUCK!"

If only, if only, if . . .

But now everything had led up to the word "duck," and that's where it started, exactly there, when he said "duck" and she turned around and looked right at him:

"Yes . . . ?"

With a questioning smile.

He stared back at her dumbly.

"Oh, sorry," she continued when she saw his surprise, "I thought . . . People often call me . . ."

He tried desperately to regain his composure, he wanted to mirror her smile, her brown eyes—but he was able to manage only a tense, strained grimace before she turned back around.

I hate myself, he thought. I always . . . I never . . . I hate myself. Now, when I had the chance, I didn't take it. Anyone would have done it, anyone. Not even Henke would have missed that opportunity, now I'll never, ever get a chance to talk to her again, he thought as tears of rage filled his eyes.

Henke continued, "Donald Duck? Are you kidding me? Not since Carl Barks . . . What is it with you, anyway? What are you staring at?"

He turned to face Henke.

He had forgotten about Henke.

He wanted to get away from Henke now. And from Spider-Man and Donald Duck.

He was glad when Henke said goodbye and hopped off the bus.

And now what?

Should he go over to her? What should he say then? Why had she turned around?

His head was spinning, and the bus was only two stops away from her stop.

He made a decision.

It's now or never, he thought.

A man's got to do what a man's got to do, he thought, getting up and practically bumping into her because she had come right over to his seat without his noticing.

"Oh . . ."

"I thought you were calling me," she said, smiling.

"Huh?"

He didn't understand.

"I thought you meant me," she said, still smiling. "When you said 'Duck.' I thought you meant me."

"Du . . . duck?" he stammered, understanding even less. "Why . . . why would I call you Duck? I would . . . I would never call you Duck."

"You wouldn't?" she said. "Why wouldn't you?"

No, now he didn't understand anything: Why was she standing here right in front of him on a tilting bus, the girl he had never talked to but had been watching for several months, the girl his heart longed for, the light of his life, why was she standing here talking about ducks?

He understood less than nothing.

"Duck? A duck is something that waddles, has a wide tail, and says quack, quack," he managed to say.

"All of those things fit me," she said cheerfully. "Quack, quack."

"Not at all," he said quickly. "You . . ."

"Yes?"

Her smile had turned into an interested smile, her brown eyes had become two inquisitive brown eyes. Now he dared to look at her and meet her gaze, and his fear and confusion vanished.

"No," he said with conviction, "you're not a duck. You're . . ."

"Yes?"

Inquisitive brown eyes.

"Well, I don't know. A squirrel . . . No. A cat, maybe. I don't know."

I don't know *yet*, he would have said if he'd been a little more audacious.

Then she said, "Cats are deceitful."

Smiling, testing.

"Not deceitful," he said. "Cats are . . ."

Then the bus got to her stop.

"Oh . . . I have to get off now."

Saved by the bell, he thought, exhaling.

In the doorway she turned toward him:

"You'll have to tell me about cats another time."

"At any rate, not a duck!" he called after her, and she waved without turning around.

And even though she was walking with her back toward him, he knew that her brown eyes were smiling.

That happened on a Thursday.

After that Thursday came the longest Friday, the longest Saturday, and the longest Sunday of his life. Of his life so far.

But Monday finally came, and he saw her waiting at the bus stop. When she got on the bus she looked around and as soon as she saw him she pushed her way through, right up to where he was sitting.

"I found this," she said and handed him a postcard.

A pale yellow postcard with a girl's face and a cat's face on it.

"No," he said decisively once he'd read the text under the pictures, "that's not what I meant. No, cats aren't that . . ."

He turned the postcard over.

"Who's Björn?"

A feeling that was new to him, a beast that he would come to know so well later on: the Green-Eyed Monster.

"A guy I know. Or a guy I knew, to be more precise," she replied.

Knew. Good, he thought. Past tense is delightful. Much better than present tense.

She stood there in silence for a minute, then she said:

"And you? What about you?"

He understood what she meant right away.

"An ostrich," he said after thinking about it for a little bit. "Or a donkey. Or a dog. A watchdog."

"Low self-esteem?" she said, smiling.

"Creative self-image," he said, smiling.

She didn't say anything else.

"So why do people call you Duck?" he asked.

"Well, they don't really call me Duck," she answered. "My name's Ann-Katrin and some people call me Ann-Ka because it sounds like 'anka.' You know, 'duck' in Swedish."

"What?"

"Ann-Ka. Ann-Katrin. Anka. Duck."

"Oh. Well, hello, Ann-Katrin," he said.

"Hello—?" she said.

He said his name.

Before he got off at Marketplace, he tried to hand the cat postcard back to her.

"You can keep it," she said. "It's yours."

"Good. Then I know what your address is," he said.

Oh, how brave he was now.

"No," she said, smiling. "You don't. Because that's my old address. I don't live there anymore."

He hopped out and the bus drove on. With her in it.

With Ann-Katrin.

And now his longing had a name.

A German grammar book

Page 93, Prepositions with Accusative and Dative.

an

Er setzt sich an den Schreibtisch.

Er sitzt am Schreibtisch.

Page 79, Modal Verbs.

Mögen

IMPERFECT

Ich mochte (du mochtest, er mochte) das Mädchen gern.

Page 51, The Helping Verb *Werden* in Future and Passive.

A) Future

Er wird in die USA fahren.

Page 17, The Four Cases of German. Strong Declension.

B) With an indefinite article.

FEMININE SINGULAR

NOM: Da läuft eine Katze.

ACC: Unser Hund jagt einer Katze.

DAT: Hast du wirklich Angst vor eine Katze?
GEN: Die Krallen einer Katze sind scharf.

He stops flipping through the German grammar book and sets it on the desk in front of him. He sighs, shakes his head, and mumbles to himself. All this stuff about trips to the USA. And cats.

After a little while he picks up the book again and calmly, systematically, rips out one page at a time and crumples each page up into a little ball that he throws at his trash can: two points, two points, two points, missed, missed, missed . . .

When all that's left is the empty cover, he has forty-eight points.

Then with a thick blue felt-tip marker he covers something that was written on the inside of the cover.

He sighs and shakes his head again because he knows that he can never cover up those numbers in his mind. They'll be written there for a long time. Forever. For as long as he's alive.

Krallen must mean claws and *scharf* must mean sharp, he thinks as he walks to the garbage chute with the cover of the German grammar book.

Then he walks back to his room.

The telephone sits where it sits. On the bookshelf. Silent.

Calling Heart's Delight

Now his bus rides were ten minutes of happiness.

Ten minutes of his bus rides were pure happiness.

Every Monday morning and Tuesday morning and Thursday morning they kept each other company on the way to school. If he succeeded in saving the seat next to him all the way to her bus stop, they sat together; otherwise they stood together. It was like being on a deserted island together in the packed bus: a sitting island or a standing island. Where they talked and talked and talked.

And laughed and giggled.

And talked and talked.

Funny. He'd always thought talking was hard.

With her it was easy.

Everything just flowed. He didn't have to search for words, he didn't come up with his responses ten minutes too late like he always did otherwise, and there were always things to talk about. So much to talk about, and the bus rides were desperately short.

It was so easy to talk to her.

He used to think that he was a T-person.

"Huh? A T-person? What's that?" she asked, curious. "Are you in some secret cult or something?"

"No, but . . . There are a lot of T words, you know. Tiresome and Tedious and Traditional and Tentative and Trivial and Tardy and . . . and Tragic and Timid and . . . I'm all of those things."

"Talk about low self-esteem!" she said, laughing and shaking her head. "You must have hit rock bottom."

"I don't have low self-esteem," he protested. "I just know myself, I—"

"Well, there're also N words," she interrupted.

"Sure. Nuisance!"

"Nice," she said.

"I know," he said. "I hate Nice."

She nodded. "Mmm. Nice is terrible."

"Mmm."

After a brief silence, she said, "Normal."

"Abnormal," he said.

"Un-abnormal," she said.

"Non-un-abnormal," he said.

"Anti-non-un-abnormal," she said.

"I give up," he said.

"Tragic," she said. "Tedious."

"Hey, I said those already," he said.

♡

27

"Okay, so you're not really nice," she said as she was about to get off the bus.

"Nice to hear."

"But not really un-nice either," she said, pursing her lips.

Ten minutes three times a week was too little, he thought. Way too little.

"Your English teacher called," his mom said one evening in a serious voice. "Miss Hammar."

"The Hammer," he mumbled, knowing what was coming.

"She said you haven't been to English class for four Wednesday mornings in a row. Well?"

He could have answered: I met a cute girl that I usually hang out with on the bus and she starts at ten o'clock on Wednesdays, so I've been forced to play hooky from English class so I can meet her. I'm sure you understand, Mom, right?

But he didn't say that. He said:

"Uh . . . uh . . . the dentist . . . Two times it was the dentist, and then there was one time when I thought we had a free period because we were supposed to go see that American movie in the evening, I'm sure you remember that, and then . . . then . . . yeah, then there was one time when I fell asleep on the bus, yeah, that was it, I didn't wake up until the last stop . . ."

His mom looked at him.

"You're lying," she said curtly.

He sat there in silence.

"Furthermore, you're lying badly," she said. But very calmly.

He didn't say anything.

"But you'll manage to make it to English class from now on, don't you think?" she said. "I don't want to get any more calls from the Hammer."

He nodded. "Of course. Definitely."

He sighed.

On the way home he rarely managed to catch the same bus she did. And sometimes when he did and saw her red hair lighting up the bus and had just started to feel that bubbling delight in his stomach, he was forced to check himself when he saw that she was with some friend from school. Even if she caught sight of him and waved happily, he would keep standing a little bit away from them and not go up to her and her friend.

He wanted to have her to himself.

There was room for only two people on their island.

But sometimes he was lucky.

Like the afternoon when he found her alone on the

bus and with an empty seat next to her, no less.

"I beg your pardon, m'lady, but is this seat taken?" he said.

"Not at all, good sir, please make yourself comfortable," she said, smiling. "Providing one keeps one's hands to oneself. I won't hear of any pawing or groping. Nor will I entertain any indecent proposals."

"Now look here, you horn dog," he said, "I certainly know—"

She interrupted him with a burst of laughter.

"You horn dog?" she said, giggling, and she composed herself. "You certainly don't mince words. Where'd you get that from?"

He shrugged his shoulders.

"My head," he said.

"Before, I was a cat," she said, smiling. "Now you're going to have to decide: Cat or dog? Maybe a sex kitten?"

Yes, she had said it herself. He thought about that the very first time he saw the movie. She'd said it herself. But then, on the bus, it was only a joke.

He didn't respond.

"I see that the lady is studying German," he said instead after a while, gesturing toward the German grammar book in her lap.

"Jawohl," she said, nodding. "And a German test tomorrow. Strong verbs. Fahren, fuhr, gefahren. Und so weiter."

"Je ne comprend pas," he said.

"Are you studying French?" she said, sounding surprised.

He nodded.

"The French language is dying out," she said. "That's what our German teacher says."

"German is a language for barbarians. That's what my French teacher says," he said, flipping through her grammar book.

He nodded.

"Mmm. She's right. This looks barbaric."

Then suddenly she stood up.

"Oh! I'm going to miss . . . I have to get off."

She pressed her way past him.

"You should liven up my bus rides more often," she said, already on her way out the door. "Bye! See you Monday!"

"Bye. Same to you," he called after her.

It wasn't until he was almost home that he discovered he was still sitting there holding her German grammar book in his hand.

D'oh! What should he do?

He sat on the edge of his bed in his room at home,

running his fingers over her book. Her name and telephone number were written on the inside of the cover.

He could reach the phone from where he was sitting.

He had to call her.

She had a German test tomorrow and needed her grammar book.

He had to call her.

He picked up the receiver, started dialing her number—and hung up the phone again.

He picked up the receiver, dialed her whole number, but quickly hung up the phone again before it could ring.

He picked up the receiver again, dialed her number, let it ring three times, and had just decided to hang up when someone answered.

It wasn't her.

It was a stranger's voice that said:

"Hello. Hello, is anyone there? Hello!"

He hung up.

His heart was pounding, his hands were sweating.

No, this wouldn't do. Was he a mouse or was he a man?

He picked up the receiver, punched in her number, and:

"Ann-Katrin," a voice in the receiver said.

"Hi, I was wondering if Ann-Katrin was home," he said, unable to interrupt the words he'd prepared.

"Are you dumb or is your bicycle just missing a few spokes?" said the voice in the receiver. "It's me, silly. I even said it was me. To whom am I speaking?"

Now he'd had a chance to collect himself.

"It's me, of course," he said. "And I have a great bicycle, thank you very much. I also have a German grammar book that I have very little use for. But I thought *you* might be missing it."

"Is it you?" she said. "I didn't recognize your phone voice. Was it you who just called a second ago?"

"I didn't recognize your phone voice either," he said.

"It was you who called before, wasn't it?" she said.

He didn't respond.

"Hello, are you still there?" she said. "It was so stupid of me to forget my grammar book. There goes my C in German. That's just like me."

"Should I come and drop the book off for you?" he said after a while. He bit his lip hard while he waited for her answer.

"Do you want to?"

Did he want to? I would pay good money for the privilege, he thought.

"Sure, no problem," he said. "I have a bike, as I mentioned. And it really would be a shame about your C in German."

"That would be so nice of you," she said.

"But I don't know where you live," he said.

She told him.

He tossed the grammar book in a grocery store bag and darted out to his bike.

I'm going to get a flat, he thought as he rode along. I'm going to be run over by a truck. I'm going to have a heart attack. I'm going to die. I'll never get there.

Sure I will. No problem.

But did she do it on purpose? Was the grammar book a dropped handkerchief? Bait that he'd swallowed? He still didn't know. He never had the courage to ask.

A potted plant

LEMON BALM, *Melissa officinalis*

Lemon balm is native to Asia. It is hardy and easy to grow. Lemon balm was cultivated by monks as a spice and ornamental plant in the Middle Ages and was significant as a medicinal herb . . .

Lemon balm makes an excellent seasoning for fish, poultry, and game dishes. Try it in broth, tea, juices, and sauces as well. Fresh lemon balm adds a delightful touch to fresh fruits and vegetables, health food, egg dishes, and salads. Tea made from lemon balm promotes good sleep and pleasant dreams.

—*Bonnier's Big Book of Gardening*

He stares at the green plant in the pot in front of him.

After hesitating for a long time, he leans forward, pinches off one of the light green leaves, crushes it between his thumb and forefinger, and holds his hand up to his nose.

Then he keeps sitting there, still again, like a statue.

But statues don't cry. And those are tears that are running down his cheeks.

Suddenly he gets up with a jerk and darts off through the apartment with the potted plant in his hand, pulls the balcony door open, and flings the pot with all his might over the edge, down toward the flower beds below.

Why does he do it?

He's breathing hard as he walks back to his desk.

Next to the desk stands the bookcase.

The bookcase stands there in silence.

The telephone too.

The scent of Heart's Delight

He looked around uneasily as he followed her into the apartment.

"Are you looking for something?"

"No, no," he said quickly, clutching his grocery store bag with sweaty hands.

"Mom works late today, she doesn't get home until after ten," she said. "If that's what you're worried about."

"No, no," he lied. "Not at all."

"Here's my room. Come on in."

He stopped in the doorway.

"I thought girls' rooms had rose-colored wallpaper. And pictures of horses. And posters of heartthrobs on their walls. And beds full of dolls and stuffed animals."

"Ah, you've obviously been in a lot of girls' rooms," she said, laughing.

"Sure, thousands," he said. "And all of them had rose-colored wallpaper and pictures of horses. But at least you have a poster of your heartthrob. You prefer older men, I see. Hello there, Leonard Cohen."

He was still standing in the doorway.

No, it wasn't true that he'd been in lots of girls' rooms. His cousin Emma's, of course. And Sara from school when she'd had a party for the class. And . . . Well, there really weren't any others. But their rooms had actually been cutesy, girly rooms. This was a normal utilitarian room, pretty much like his own.

"Do you play?" He nodded toward a guitar case that was leaning against the wall.

"Mmm-hmm. But come in and sit down now. Or are you afraid?"

"Pshah," he sniffed. "After all, I've been in thousands of girls' rooms."

There was a chair and the bed to choose from.

She sat down on the chair.

Now the bed was the only choice left, and he sat down carefully, carefully, on the very edge of her bed.

She looked at him, amused:

"Are you afraid of wrinkling the bedspread?"

"Yeah, right," he said and flung himself backward. "After all, I've sat on thousands of girls' beds."

"And lain in thousands too, I suppose," she said.

"There've been a few, yes," he lied.

"I can believe that, yes." She smiled.

♡

Talking and talking and talking and laughing and a cup of tea and the evening flew by and he couldn't understand it, he couldn't comprehend it.

He was in her home. It was him and her. In her home. How had it happened? How had he ended up here? He couldn't understand it.

And he talked and talked and laughed and ten o'clock had never arrived so early.

"Yikes! I have to go home now."

"So you are a little afraid of my mom after all, aren't you?" she teased.

"Oh, hardly," he lied. "I've met thousands of girls' mothers. But my bike turns into a pumpkin at ten o'clock."

"Don't forget to lose your glass slipper on the way out," she said, laughing.

He got up from the bed.

In the window he discovered five potted plants with light green leaves that were all more or less identical.

"What kind of plant do you have in the window?"

"Come here," she said.

She pinched two leaves off one of the plants and gave one of them to him.

"Do like this," she said and crushed her leaf between her thumb and index finger.

He did as she said. "And now what?"

Then she took his hand carefully in hers and guided it up under his nose.

STOP!

Can we have that sequence again, in slow motion and with closeups:

She—took—his hand—in hers—and—her hand—was—soft—and—slightly warm.

The First Touch. Thank you.

PROCEED:

"Smell!"

He smelled. Mmm. It smelled like lemons, so fresh and good and strong.

"Mmmm . . ."

She had let go of his hand and was looking at him contentedly.

"Smells good, doesn't it?"

He nodded happily.

"What is it? Some kind of forbidden drug?"

"Heart's delight," she responded.

"What?"

"Heart's delight. It's an herb. It's called heart's delight. Or lemon balm. But heart's delight is prettier, don't you think?"

"Definitely," he said.

But he furrowed his brow.

"What is it?" she asked.

"I recognize that scent. I was just trying to think of where I've smelled it before . . ."

She smiled to herself but said nothing. Then:

"Why don't you take one? If you want. I mean, I have five of them. I planted them myself. You can use the leaves in salads. Or make tea out of them. It promotes good sleep and pleasant dreams."

"Sure. I'd like one. Sure."

He took the pot she was handing him.

"I can put it here in my bag."

"Bye."

"Bye. And thanks for the heart's delight."

"Uh-huh. You're welcome."

Silence. But he didn't budge.

"Be careful you don't drown," she said, and he looked up, startled.

"Oh, sorry. I was hypnotized," he said.

"You have nice eyes," she said.

How do you respond to something like that? In three seconds he thought of twenty different responses, but went with:

"Yours aren't exactly butt-ugly either."

"Boy, you really know how to take a compliment. And give one." She sighed but looked pleased nonetheless. "It definitely shows that you've been with thousands of girls."

He nodded.

"I'll go home and dream pleasant dreams now," he said.

"Good luck," she said.

"Bye."

"Bye."

Now he had to go.

He broke free from the spell.

He left.

He passed a redheaded woman on the stairs.

It wasn't until he took the potted plant out in his room at home that he discovered he'd brought her German grammar book home with him again.

He laughed out loud.

"Heart's delight," he whispered to himself. "That's what you are . . ."

A page from a songbook

Out in our garden blueberries grow
Come heart's delight
If you want to be with me,
come meet me there
Come lilies and columbine
Come roses and sage
Come sweet mint, come heart's delight

Fine little flowers invite us to dance
Come heart's delight
If you wish, I'll bind you a wreath
Come lilies . . .

With this wreath, I'll adorn your hair
Come heart's delight
The sun is setting but hope is nigh
Come lilies . . .

Out in our garden are blossoms and berries
Come heart's delight

But most of all you are dearest to me
Come lilies . . .

He hums softly as he reads. Then he stops humming and tears the page into thin strips; he tears each strip into four pieces and rolls each piece into a little ball that he stuffs into his mouth.

It takes him four minutes to eat the Swedish folk song "Uti Vår Hage." On the bookshelf the telephone sits just as silently as before. Almost more silently.

Come Heart's Delight

"He's so boring," sighed Henke.

"Mmm."

"And yet he thinks he's so enormously interesting."

"Mmm."

"What's he talking about?" Henke asked.

"National romanticism."

It was Art and Music History class, and he and Henke were sitting at the very back of the room. The music teacher, a relic from the 60s, stood at the board and talked and talked. As usual he was dressed in a checked shirt and jeans. Always the same checked shirt.

"You're familiar, quite familiar, with this song, 'Uti Vår Hage,' for example," he continued, "and it is an unusually clear example of how . . ."

"I just can't take any more," groaned Henke, "he—"

"Shh! Be quiet for a second, I want to hear this!"

Henke was looking at him in astonishment, but he leaned forward and tried to concentrate on what their music teacher was saying up there. He had discovered some familiar words in the song's lyrics that the music teacher had put up on the overhead.

The words were: *heart's delight.*

". . . now, if you look at these lyrics, this appears to be a beautiful, poetic love song, just the type of song people were looking for in their hunt for things that were authentically Swedish, because when they were out among the common people and transcribing songs and melodies, well, at least half of the songs were far too lewd and indecent, and that wouldn't do for the overall national . . . uh . . . for this type of typical . . . Swedish cultural heritage that people wanted to write down and preserve, and also use in people's parlors, uh . . . So quite a bit of the material was censored, but this song, 'Uti Vår Hage,' a Swedish folk song from Gotland, it was beautiful and inoffensive and spread quickly and became very popular. But . . ."

Henke groaned.

"Shh! I want to hear this!"

". . . but actually a bit of traditional women's knowledge slipped through as this song circulated, and that knowledge is not at all as pure and innocent as one might at first think. Now take a look at these lyrics here. The refrain is a list of plants: lilies and columbine and roses, those are flowers. And sage and mint are herbs, and heart's delight is actually also an herb that is also called—"

"Lemon balm!"

Our music teacher looked up in surprise. "Yes, exactly. A very useful herb that gives off a strong scent of—"

"Lemon!"

"Exactly, yes . . . yes, that's obvious from the name, heh heh, but what's interesting about all of these plants here and what the national romantics weren't aware of when they circulated this beautiful song is that they were used as abortifacients. For abortions, in other words. The plants, that is."

Up by the board he stood quietly for a moment.

"Is he waiting for us to applaud?" Henke muttered. "When did you get to be such an expert on herbs?"

"Shh!"

"So, the point I wanted to make, then, is that this beautiful love song, one of Sweden's most beloved and widespread folk songs, as a matter of fact, is a list of abortifacients, of different ways of terminating an unwanted pregnancy, and in the old agricultural socie—"

"Couldn't we sing it now?" interrupted some of the girls.

"Yes, certainly we can," said the music teacher.

"In two parts?"

"Let's take the melody together first," their music teacher said, sitting down at the piano.

He told her about it the next morning on the bus.

She laughed.

"So, heart's delight can be used for that too. Hmm . . ."

"At least that's what our music teacher says. But I wouldn't rely on him if I were a girl."

"Zum Tango gehören zwei," she said and smiled an earnest smile.

"Huh?"

"It takes two to tango."

"Thanks," he said, "I understood that. But . . ."

"Oh, never mind," she said. "Do you want to come and bring me my German grammar book tonight? My mom's working."

"On the subject of tango . . ."

"Don't get any ideas. Are you coming?"

"Sure."

The German grammar book had become a standing joke. Their password. A shared memory. He still had it at home and didn't even take it with him anymore when he went to her place.

The German grammar book was his hostage.

But he went to her place. Not often, but sometimes. And he'd successfully avoided her redheaded mother. Everyone else too, for that matter. He met her on the bus or at her place, never anywhere else, and never together with anyone else.

This was a two-person game he was playing, not some multi-player game.

And the talk about sex was just talk, nothing else. He had still only sat on her bed.

They were friends, they talked and laughed together, he got goose bumps when he thought about her, he could drown in her eyes, but they were Adam and Eve before the apple.

Yes, that's for sure. That's true.

He had never kissed her. He had never thought about . . . about her body. That's for sure. That's true.

He couldn't have said whether she had large or small breasts.

He slept with his hands on top of the blankets.

Yes, that's true.

That's how it still was then.

A record

He sits with an album cover in front of him, and a record is spinning on the record player.

He listens to the song one last time:

stepping out of the grey day she came
her red hair falling like the sky
love held them there in that moment with
     the whole world passing by

he could look through all of his books
and not find a line that would do
to tell of changes he could feel her make in him
just by being there

so good just to walk in the light
may the moon shine down on love every night
sometimes it seems the only things real
are what we are and what we feel
               — "Red Hair"
          Lyrics & Music: Mike Heron

"*Liquid Acrobat as Regards the Air*," he says to himself. Hell of a name for an album. Typical Dad. Damn . . .

He has tears in his eyes.

"Damn damn damn . . ."

He takes the record off the record player and lets the needle scrape over its surface.

Once he's put the record on his desk, he takes out his Swiss army knife, flips out the biggest knife blade, and carves long, deep notches into the record. He cuts as if he were dividing a cake into twelve slices. Calmly and methodically. Almost carefully. And then the same on the other side. There, cake for twelve. Now no one can ever listen to the Incredible String Band's album *Liquid Acrobat as Regards the Air* again.

He takes the record to the balcony too, and from there he throws it like a frisbee out into the summer night. It rises first like a flying saucer and then slowly and gently falls down over the parking lot, finally landing on the roof of a car.

As he follows the record's journey, he realizes that he is standing there with his knife in his hand. He throws it as well.

"Hey, Switzerland! Stupid crappy country. Stupid crappy knife."

He folds the album cover in two and flings it down the garbage chute, then sits down at his desk again.

"Damn damn damn . . ."

Surely he didn't need to be swearing this much?

But the telephone there on the bookshelf says nothing at all.

It sits there in silence.

Heart's Delight offers him the apple

Dad hadn't left much behind when he moved out: one pile of records, one mom with her eyes red from crying, and one wide-eyed six-year-old who didn't understand anything.

Why was Dad moving? He and Mom never used to argue or fight, they didn't scream at each other, and they never hit each other the way he'd seen moms and dads do on TV sometimes.

They were a regular family that ate breakfast together every morning and watched TV together every evening.

And they'd taken a car trip to Norway together, for vacation.

They were a regular family.

A happy family.

Anyway, that's how he liked to remember it now, ten years later.

And never in his life had he felt so deceived as when Dad moved out. And never so empty: If he were to wake up in the middle of the night and shout "Dad," who would come now? Who would tuck him in, give him a little kiss, sing a little song?

No one.

Because Dad had moved in with some lady.

Never before in his life had he felt so deceived and so empty.

He had more experience with deceit now. Twice as much.

It wasn't until Krister moved in with Mom and him, and his completely adorable little half-sister Hanna came along, that he started thinking about Dad again. Before, he had just wanted to forget Dad.

It wasn't that Krister was an evil stepfather or anything, not at all, it was just that Krister was a different kind of person. Dad must have been my kind, he thought. Dad is in me, half of me is Dad. At least.

So he started wondering about Dad. Could he get to know Dad now? Would it be possible to understand him?

That Dad was a Loser, that he understood. Dad had left Mom and him for the Love of His Life ten years ago, he knew that now, but after just half a year the Love of His Life got tired of Dad and moved to Vännäs.

How had Dad felt then? Vännäs, of all places . . .

Yes, Dad was a Loser.

But all the same: It was time to try to get to know Dad now. So he started searching for his father.

First he searched in the stack of records.

The music Dad had left behind. A bunch of groups he'd

never heard of: Incredible String Band, Jefferson Airplane, Country Joe and the Fish, Fairport Convention, Grateful Dead. Shrill British folk music and American hippie rock.

He listened and read the lyrics.

It didn't add up. There was philosophy and mysticism and revolution and LSD and religion and nursery rhymes and anti-war protests. A mishmash.

No, he didn't get a lot of help from the records in his search for his dad.

But he found a song called "Red Hair."

And since that was right when he discovered a girl with red hair on the bus, a girl who lit up his bus rides, well, you know, he listened to it and read the lyrics and listened to it again

and again

and again

and again

and it was about her. And about him. Exactly.

The record was already scratched and warped to begin with, and now by the end of May it sounded like something from that radio program that played the old 78s.

But he continued to listen:

Every day he listened to the song about the girl with the red hair, the one who changed him just by being there.

♡

And then one evening she was there.

"There's a young woman here looking for you," Mom said one evening with a knowing look.

A young woman?

He went out into the hall, and there she stood.

She was just standing there and she said:

"I was out going for a walk. It was such a nice evening. And then I thought that I might drop by. After all, you have a German grammar book of mine, don't you? We have a German test tomorrow, so I probably ought to have it."

With red cheeks and his heart rejoicing he stood silently, staring at her. Finally he said:

"Good. Cool. Sure, come in. The woman standing there staring is my mom. She's harmless. And this is Ann–Katrin."

". . . and she's extremely dangerous," Ann–Katrin herself added, greeting Mom graciously.

"Welcome," Mom said. "Come in, Ann–Katrin. Do you know each other from school, or—?"

"No," he said abruptly and pulled Ann–Katrin along with him. "Here's my room, come on."

"Should I make a little tea for you guys?" Mom called after them.

"No thanks," he said.

"Yes please," Ann–Katrin said. "That would be nice."

"You're not mad that I came here, are you?" she asked.

"No, no, it's just my mom, she's so nosy . . ."

"She's not used to women coming to visit you?"

"Yeah, yeah, thousands of girls come through here, it's not that . . ."

"What are you listening to?"

He quickly shut off the amplifier. "I'll show you later. We can listen later. It's my dad's old record. One of the ones he left behind."

"Are they divorced?"

"Mmm–hmm. He left ten years ago."

"Mine left when I was thirteen," she said. "I'd just started eighth grade. But it was just as well. Mom is much happier now. And him too."

He looked at her in surprise. Could that be?

"Don't you see your dad?" she asked.

He shook his head. "It was years ago. But this summer, maybe. I don't know. I didn't want to see him . . . before . . ."

She didn't say anything.

"Couldn't we talk about something else," he said.

She nodded. "I see you have your heart's delight in the window there."

"Mmm. And in here," he said and tapped on his own heart.

She didn't let on that she understood.

Mom brought tea and nice sandwiches on a tray, and the evening flew by.

Heart's Delight always made the time fly by.

"There was some music you were going to play for me," she said. "I have to go home soon."

"Mmm. Just this one song."

He put the record on and handed her the album cover.

"Red Hair . . ."

She listened with concentration, and then said:

"Mmm. Weird music. But nice. Cool with the cello. Cool."

"I've listened to it . . . a lot," he mumbled. "I like the lyrics."

Then she got serious all of a sudden and looked at him seriously and said in a serious voice:

"You mustn't—"

She couldn't say it. But he should have understood it anyway.

He didn't want to understand.

He didn't even notice it.

When she got up to go she tried again:

"You mustn't . . . You mustn't . . . You . . ."

"Mmm?"

Then she sighed and gave up. "Come here."

And then she gave him a hug.

And then it was exactly the opposite.

Because once she'd gone he was left standing in the middle of the floor feeling her soft body imprinted against his own. Now it hadn't been two friends saying goodbye, it had been her belly against his, her thighs against his, her chest against his, her hair against his cheek. And his lips almost against her neck. Almost.

It was exactly the opposite.

That she had tried to tell him something, something important, a few minutes ago . . . he didn't think about that.

He hadn't even noticed it.

He didn't notice it until the third time he watched the movie, and then of course it was too late.

Something else happened that evening. Something began. He didn't sleep with his hands on top of the covers anymore. Thanks for the yummy apple! Thank you, dear serpent.

An empty plastic box

Is it really empty, the plastic box he's sitting and staring at? He takes off the lid, moves the box around in front of him, holds it out his window and shakes it.

Then he goes out to the kitchen and washes it carefully. Smells it, wrinkles his nose, casts a glance at the container of dishwashing liquid: Aha! Lemon-fresh scent.

He washes it carefully and for a long time before he's satisfied.

Was it really empty?

In his room, the telephone continues to sit silently.

Relics from Heart's Delight

"True, I usually nag you to clean your room, but aren't you going a little overboard now?"

Mom had opened the door to his room and discovered him crawling around on the floor with a pair of tweezers in his hand. That was the day after Ann-Katrin's visit. The day after Heart's Delight was in his room. The day after the hug.

"Haven't I told you to knock?" he said angrily. "Haven't I said that? Well?"

"What are you doing?" asked his mom, curious.

He didn't answer, just slammed the door shut in front of her face.

But what *was* he doing?

Looking for relics.

It had started with him finding a long strand of red hair on his desk. He smelled it:

A faint, faint hint of lemon. Maybe.

He carefully poked the strand of hair down into a little plastic box, and started looking for more.

On the rug he found another one. And another one.

That was when his mom opened the door.

After he had searched his room from floor to ceiling he had seven strands of red hair in the box. He stuffed it under his pillow. Those were his relics from Heart's Delight.

On the bus she was the same as ever.

There was no noticeable difference in her. It was as if nothing special had happened.

"When was it that you were going to America?" she asked.

"On the last day of school. Right after school. But I don't want to anymore. To go, that is."

"No? Why not?"

She looked really surprised. Didn't she get it? He wanted to be with her, of course. He did not at all want to live with a family in America for a whole long month. Didn't she get that?

"Uh..." was all he said.

"Where are you going?"

"Boston, Massachusetts," he answered. "Or outside of Boston, to be exact. A place called Marblehead."

"Oh, I see. For a month, you said."

"What will you be doing then?" he asked. "Something besides studying German?"

She laughed. "Relaxing. Sleeping in. Staying up late. Nothing special. And then I have a guest coming. A . . . someone I met last winter. And then I'm going sailing with my dad for two weeks. Along the Norrland coast."

STOP THERE!

She'd said it! She had actually said it!

And he'd missed it.

She said: And then I have a guest coming. And he hadn't thought any more about it.

He didn't ask: Who's coming?

He didn't ask: Is your guest a boy or a girl?

He missed it, but she had actually said it.

He didn't notice that until the third or fourth time he watched the movie.

Probably he missed it because she continued:

"And I hope there'll be time to see you some too . . ."

He nodded, pleased. That was what he'd wanted to hear.

"We could keep riding the bus every morning," he said, laughing. "Every Monday and Tuesday and Thursday, at least. Even though it's summer vacation. It would seem empty otherwise."

"Not on your life," she said, laughing too.

A pack of condoms

From the balcony, light oblong balloons sail out into the night. One, two, three, four of them lift off and waft away in the warm breeze.

And he sits on the floor of the balcony, blowing up the fifth condom into a blimp, and there, yes, now *Hindenburg V* lifts off too.

He dries his sticky fingers off on his pants.

That'll do, he thinks. I can find something else to do with the five that are left.

Then he has an idea.

He goes into the apartment and gets a pin from next to his mom's sewing machine. Then he carefully sticks it through the little wrapper around the first condom.

He looks at his work. It doesn't show on the outside. Good.

He nods in satisfaction and then punctures the four remaining condoms, puts them back in the pack, stuffs the pack in a brown envelope, and writes on the envelope:

HAVE A NICE TIME.

I know who should get this letter, he thinks and laughs wickedly.

He nods to himself. Maybe I've given someone life, he thinks.

He thinks for a minute.

Maybe I've given someone death too, he thinks, but shrugs his shoulders and goes back to his room.

After he shoves the envelope into the bottom drawer of his desk, he leans back in his chair and shuts his eyes.

The movie continues and
the phone continues
to sit silently.

Preparing for Heart's Delight

It can't have been a coincidence. Not everything.

There must have been a reason that it happened.

Someone must have intended for it to happen.

Someone must have written the screenplay. But who?
It can't have been a coincidence

that her mom started working nights at the hospital in
June and

that the last day of school was a Monday this year for
the first time in the history of the world and

that Mom and Krister and Hanna went to the cabin the
last weekend before summer vacation and

that he stayed home to pack before his America trip and

that he ran into her on the bus on the way home from
school on precisely that Friday and

that she said her mom would be working or sleeping all
weekend and

that he said he was home alone for the whole weekend and

that she said:

"I'm going to a party tonight. But I could come over to

your place tomorrow night. It would be silly for my German grammar book to lie around cluttering up your house all summer. Since you'll be in America and everything. So I could take this opportunity to come get it. Or do you have other plans?"

No, there were way too many factors. It can't all have been coincidence.

But who was it that was writing the screenplay? And for what reason? Was there a reason?

"Or do you have other plans?"

"Tomorrow night?"

He pretended to contemplate the question.

"No . . . No, nothing special . . ."

And she said:

"Then I'll come sometime after eight. After Mom goes to work."

"Okay, good," he said.

And she hopped off the bus, and he decided to buy a pack of condoms.

Just to be safe.

He had never bought a pack of condoms before. Certainly no one worries about buying a pack of condoms these days? Certainly there can't be anyone who thinks it's embarrassing?

Why would it be embarrassing? Something completely natural. Kids learn in junior high how good condoms are. And how important.

Buying a pack of condoms is as easy as buying a carton of milk. You just go into the store, take what you want, and pay at the cash register.

Bye, Mom, I'm just going to pop down and buy a pack of condoms for the weekend.

You should be able to say that to your mom. Something completely natural.

He sighed.

All afternoon he'd been trying to convince himself that it was a completely natural thing to do, just a normal purchase, nothing even worth thinking about.

Now he was standing in the grocery store and comparing the prices on different shampoos, studying razor blades and shaving cream, and imperceptibly inching slowly closer to where the packs of condoms were hanging.

Already, right when he'd gotten home from school, he'd biked over to a newsstand where he knew there was a vending machine that sold condoms, because even if it was just as normal now to buy condoms as it was to buy skim milk, it still seemed easier to just slip a couple of coins into a dispenser and get what you wanted. Without having to say anything, and without anyone seeing you.

Of course someone had broken the machine and plundered its contents.

Then he'd been to three different neighborhood grocery stores in a row—the ICA, the Minilivs, and the Närköpet—but all three places kept the condoms by the cash register with the cigarettes and tobacco, so you were forced to go up to the cashier and say:

"Ahem. Oh, and I'd like a pack of those too."

Or:

"Which of those brands of condoms over there is the best? What type do you use? Ah, I see, well then, I'll take one of the blue packs . . . How much are they?"

Or something like that.

But

at the ICA the cashier was very cute and very female and

at the Minilivs the cashier knew his mom and

at the Närköpet a girl from his class came and got in line behind him just as he was about to make his move. He quickly changed his plans:

"A pack . . . uh . . . a pack of Marlboros."

"Did you start smoking?" his classmate asked.

"Oh, just at parties. I'm going to a party tonight," he lied.

"Oh."

Which is why he was now standing in his fourth grocery store, Konsum, holding a shopping basket in his hand and slowly but surely inching his way toward the condoms. In his basket there was a bag of chips, a bag of Cheez Doodles, and a carton of milk.

Now. Now he was standing right in front of the condoms. A quick glance to the right, a quick glance to the left, and then he grabbed a pack and poked it down under the bag of chips.

Yep. Easy as pie.

Now all he had to do was pay.

The cashier was a man. Good.

Easy as pie.

But . . .

He stopped and set the basket down. What if he got up there . . . and put everything on the conveyor belt:

a bag of chips

a carton of milk

a bag of Cheez Doodles

a pack of condoms.

What if the cashier smiled knowingly, winked at him, and said:

"Ah, so you're going to do a little dipping tonight."

He sighed, walked back into the aisles, and swore under his breath:

"Damn damn damn."

He couldn't do this.

Young people in Sweden in the 1990s think it's completely natural and normal to buy condoms at Konsum.

He wasn't normal.

With sweaty palms he walked to the health food aisle. He set his basket on the floor in front of the brown rice and dried lentils, squatted down, cast a quick glance around, and stuffed the pack of condoms into his jacket.

He left the basket and walked back toward the exit.

To keep the cashier from suspecting anything he bought an evening paper.

"Anything else?"

"No thanks."

So that was that.

Easy as pie.

Now he had a pack of condoms. There really wasn't anything extraordinary about it, was there?

Now he was prepared.

A sheet

What is he doing now? Pretending to be a ghost?

He's sitting on his bed with a sheet over his head. There are strange noises coming from in there. Is he crying again? If he keeps this up, he might end up in *The Guinness Book of World Records*: Most tears shed in one night.

He's already cried two buckets full. And the sad part of the movie hasn't even started yet.

Why is a sheet making him cry?

What kinds of smells does he notice under the sheet there? Does he notice the smell of two sweaty people? Of sweat and other fluids that can come out of the human body?

Does he smell a faint scent of lemon?

Now he pulls the sheet off himself and lays it on the floor. He stands still, staring at it.

What does he see? Does he see the imprint of a naked body? Does he see the imprint of two naked bodies? Does he see any stains? Blood, sweat, and tears?

Nope, no blood.

It wasn't the first time for *both* of them.

He closes his eyes and nods. Now he's ready. How do you get rid of a sheet? he thinks. You could burn it. Cut it to pieces. Tear it to shreds. Throw it in . . .

Washing it will do, he thinks. That'll do. So he takes the sheet down to the laundry room in the basement. Who does laundry on a Saturday night? No one.

No one besides him.

He bunches the sheet up and stuffs it into the washing machine, fills the dispenser to the brim with detergent, and turns the dial to whites, to hot.

There.

Water starts pouring in and the machine starts to hum.

Wash, washing machine, wash! Wash away all the memories of what took place on that sheet.

Can a sheet remember?

Then wash away the sheet's memory, he thinks. Wash it until it's blindingly white and blank.

The phone has been silent while he's been in the laundry room. It continues to be silent once he sits back down at his desk again.

Oh, Heart's Delight, oh

Couldn't we just fast-forward over this part?

No! It has to be the whole movie. The full, uncensored version.

But this one is the hardest scene for him to watch. All the same, it's the scene he's watched the most times. It's also the part that kept the movie from getting a PG–13 rating.

She came.

Saturday night finally came, the doorbell rang, he let it ring twice before he opened the door, and there she stood.

"Hi," she said, coming in. "What did you do today?"

He could have answered:

6:37 a.m. Got up. Even though I was the only one home and it was Saturday.

7:12 a.m. Finished packing for America trip.

7:34 a.m. Breakfast. Yogurt as usual.

8:52 a.m. Thought: She won't come after all. It was just

something she said. She didn't really mean it. She's already forgotten that she said it.

9:25 a.m. Thought: She definitely won't come. I might as well quit waiting. She won't come.

10:03 a.m. Tried to listen to the Swedish "Top 10" countdown.

10:21 a.m. Turned off the radio.

10:22 a.m. Started counting the cars that drove by on the street below the window. Made tables with the different car colors. White won, of course. Ahead of red. White and red were the winners.

1:50 p.m. Ate two bananas.

2:03 p.m. Went to the bathroom.

3:45 p.m. Flipped on the TV and tried to watch an old black-and-white Swedish movie starring Julia Caesar.

4:06 p.m. Turned off the TV.

4:20 p.m. Counted cars again. Unusually high number of black ones.

5:11 p.m. Made a nice diagram of the car color statistics.

5:50 p.m. Checked my passport and visa. Thought I looked like a juvenile delinquent in the passport photo.

6:15 p.m. Heated up some food that Mom had taken out of the freezer for me. "Indonesian Pork Curry, 2 servings," it said on the plastic container.

6:29 p.m. Ate it. Pretty good.

6:35 p.m. Washed the dishes.

6:47 p.m. Sat on a stool in the hallway. Thought: She won't come after all.

7:47 p.m. Went on sitting. Thought: She definitely won't come.

8:00 p.m. Thought: If she's not here in fifteen minutes, she's definitely not coming.

8:15 p.m. Thought: She gets five more minutes.

8:19 p.m. The doorbell rang. I raced to the door but waited a little bit before opening it.

Yeah, that's what he could have answered.

He could also have said:

"I waited and waited."

He wouldn't have been lying either. But he said:

"I packed my stuff for America. And . . . well . . ."

She nodded and walked into his room ahead of him. She sat down and made herself comfortable on his bed, pulling her knees up under her chin.

"Well." She smiled.

He was quiet. For once her presence didn't elicit a whole flood of words from him. All the words were gone.

"This seems really dangerous." She smiled again. "Alone with a young man in an empty apartment. And a Saturday night, no less. My mom warned me about this kind of thing."

He was even quieter. It was so quiet in the room that a pin falling on the floor would have sounded like a gunshot.

She smiled at his silence.

She smiled a Mona Lisa smile.

He had put the pack of condoms under his pillow. That all seemed as distant as the Andromeda galaxy right now.

But the spell was broken. His paralysis dissipated.

It started with an irritating laugh:

"Did you eat googly-eye soup for dinner or something?"

"Huh? Ahem," he croaked. "No . . . Indonesian pork curry, but nothing else . . . umm . . . and two bananas . . ."

"Actually I didn't eat much today," she said. "And suddenly I'm starving. Maybe we could make something to eat?"

"Sure," he said, finding his tongue again. "Tea and sandwiches at least. I make the best tea in town."

"And I bake the best scones in Sweden," she said happily.

"And we have the best black currant jam in Scandinavia in the fridge."

"And I won the Olympic medal in napkin folding. I can fold the Dying Swan with my eyes closed."

"If you'll bake the scones and fold the napkins, I'll make the tea and open the jam. Come on."

They raced out to the kitchen together.

One hour later they were sitting directly across from each other at the dining table.

"Mmm. I can see why you won a medal for your scones. Delicious! Mmm," he said, brushing some crumbs off his cheek. "But I'm a little disappointed in that swan. It looks more like a . . . a . . . well, a crumpled-up napkin."

"Wrong kind of napkins," she said with her mouth full of jam and scone. "Wrong color. I can't fold red swans."

Two hours later they were still sitting directly across from each other at the dining table. Talking and laughing and talking and laughing and talking.

Three hours later he said:

"Maybe we should clean up a little."

"You go right ahead," she said. "And I'll sit here and watch."

She hopped up on the counter and sat there dangling her legs while he cleared the table, gathered up crumbs, and started to do the dishes. While she watched him, her Mona Lisa smile came back.

"You're cute when you do dishes."

"Right," he mumbled, rinsing out the sponge.

"No really, it's true," she said. "You're so cute I could eat you up."

"Right."

"Come here," she said.

Something had happened to her voice. The change was very slight, but he noticed it.

"Come here," she said again and he went over and stood in front of her.

She spread her knees apart to make room for him.

"Come closer," she whispered. "Come closer so I can taste you."

The first of many kisses.

The first time their lips got to touch. The first time their tongues got to greet each other. The first time their teeth bumped up against each other.

"Mmm." She nodded contentedly. "You taste good, too."

He didn't want to talk now. Now he wanted to kiss.

And kiss and kiss and kiss and kiss and kiss.

"Take it easy," she said with her hand on his cheek. "I need to breathe a little too. Calm down."

He nodded dumbly and stretched a little. "Uh. I strained my neck. Ahh . . ."

"Poor ergonomics," she said, smiling.

"Mmm . . ."

"Maybe we could go to your room," she said. "There wouldn't necessarily be anything too dangerous in that . . ."

He shook his head eagerly.

"Come on!" She took his hand and pulled him back to his room. There she hopped up and sat on his bed again, but he stopped in his tracks and stood still in front of her.

She was sitting on his pillow.

Swish, faster than the speed of light, the blue pack of condoms was catapulted into outer space. It was almost here and yet still infinitely far away.

"A penny for your thoughts," she said, smiling.

"Okay. But the money first," he said, smiling and stretching out his hand.

She pulled him toward her.

"Come here. I'll massage your sore neck."

"Kiss me first," he said.

But she didn't kiss him. She put her hands on his cheeks and looked at him with a serious look in her eyes.

"This is a mistake," she said.

He shook his head.

"Yes, this is a mistake," she said.

He nodded. "Okay then, it's a mistake. Now kiss me."

The strange thing was, he thought afterward, that it didn't feel strange. Nothing felt strange that evening.

Everything made perfect sense.

He thought that was strange. Afterward. When he watched the movie. And when he watched the movie he also noticed what she said about its being a mistake.

As she massaged his neck, her fingers started exploring other parts of his body.

And his fingers began to explore her body. It was a new experience for his fingers.

She was soft. And in some places she was a little moist.

He started to take off her clothes.

She started to take off his clothes.

Soon they had taken off each other's clothes.

She was so soft and a little moist.

"I guess it was dangerous after all," she said, holding him out away from herself with her hands on his shoulders. "I should have listened to my mother."

"I'm completely harmless," he said, wanting to continue with what he'd been doing.

"Oh? So what's that that's sticking up there then?" she said with a nod.

He glanced down below his belly.

"Oh, that. He's completely harmless too," he said and tried to tip her over onto the bed.

"Wait a second," she said, slipping away from him. "I have to pee first. Too much tea . . ."

Once she left the room, he pulled the bedspread off the bed and crawled under the covers.

Here I am, lying in my bed waiting for Heart's Delight, he thought.

It doesn't feel strange at all, he thought.

Under his head, under his pillow, was a pack of condoms. It had touched down now.

And then she came to him, and crawled into the bed next to him, and opened herself to him, and . . .

"But . . . but," he stuttered and pulled away from her.

He sat up and ran his index finger over her stomach, drew a ring around her belly button, and another one and another one.

"What is it?" she asked.

Her head on the pillow.

"What . . . what about . . . what about getting . . . getting pregnant?" he stammered, not daring to look into her eyes.

She laughed. But not in a mean way.

She laughed in a nice way and said:

"Well, I think you're safe. I mean, women can get

pregnant, but I've never heard of a man getting pregnant. But let me show you something."

She rolled out of bed, went over to the window, and pulled up the shade.

"What do you see?" she asked with her back turned toward him.

"You," he said happily. "And you have no clothes on."

She turned toward him.

"Hmm . . . you don't seem to have any clothes on either. But you're supposed to look at the sky. What do you see?"

He looked out at the night sky.

"A moon," he said. "That is completely full."

"Exactly." She nodded. "A full moon. And when there's a full moon, I'm at my least fertile. I know my body. I can't get pregnant when there's a full moon. It's biologically impossible. Trust me."

Trust her? If she'd said that he could fly he'd have opened the window and flung himself out.

She pulled down the blind again and came over to him.

"And if you're afraid of girl cooties," she said seriously, "I don't have any. And you . . . I presume you don't have any boy cooties to infect me with . . ."

"No, no . . ."

Seven seconds. Silence and thoughts.

"Come on then," she said then. "What are you waiting for?"

Farewell, condoms. You can leave Gaea and hie thee hence to the next galaxy. Five, four, three, two, one, zero . . .

The first time.

The first time in his life.

And it was over in five seconds.

"Oh . . ."

He couldn't bear to look at her.

"Sorry," he mumbled with his face in the pillow.

She turned his face toward her and looked at him closely.

"Hey, silly," she said lovingly. "What are you apologizing for? It takes a little time to get to know each other, to get to know each other this way, I mean. It just takes a little time . . ."

He nodded.

He wanted nothing more than to get to know her. In this way.

"You're so adorable," she said and let her fingers rest against his lips.

Adorable?

Had anyone ever told him that he was adorable?

He thought about it.

Mom maybe, when he was a little baby and she was

washing him in the bathtub, supporting his heavy head in her one hand.

Had she said, "You're so adorable"?

Maybe. But he didn't know it. He couldn't remember.

"You're so adorable," she whispered again.

He liked it.

It made him feel warm.

And he said the only thing there was to say:

"You're the one who's adorable."

And he meant it.

"You're so soft," she said and let her fingers continue along his neck, down to his shoulders and chest. "You're so soft, like a baby."

"You're the one who's soft," he said.

And he meant it.

She was so adorable and soft, unlike anyone else.

So adorable and soft and a little moist.

"What is it?"

He wriggled out of the bed without a word and walked over to the window.

"What are you doing?" she asked.

He didn't say anything until he was back next to her in the bed.

"Heart's delight," he said then and held up a few leaves

he'd picked from the plant on the windowsill. Heart's delight for Heart's Delight. He rubbed a couple of leaves between his fingers and then stroked the skin behind her left ear.

And without saying a word he anointed her carefully and with great seriousness

under her chin
and on her left shoulder
and on her left breast
and on her stomach
and on her left hip
and on her left knee
and on all the toes on her left foot
and on all the toes on her right foot
and on her right knee
and on her right hip
and on her stomach again
and on her right breast
and on her right shoulder
and under her chin again
and finally behind her right ear.

She lay still on her back the whole time. Only when he was finished did she lift her head from the pillow and say, giggling:

"What are you doing? Are you planning to eat me up? Now that you've seasoned me . . ."

"Mmm," he said, nodding. And kissed her toes and her knees and her hips and her stomach and her breasts and her shoulders and her chin. Finally he kissed her behind her ears. "Mmm. You taste like lemons."

"Sour like a lemon?" She smiled.

"Good like a lemon," he said.

"Do you know what the first thing I noticed about you was?" he asked after a little while.

She nodded.

"After your hair then?" he said.

She shook her head.

"Your ear," he said.

"My ear? I have two of them, you know. You noticed only one of them?" she asked, amused.

"Mmm." He nodded. "It was the right one. That one."

"Hmm . . . Do you know what the first thing I noticed about you was?" she asked.

"No."

"That you were always staring at me on the bus. I thought: That guy, he must have eaten googly-eye soup for breakfast . . ."

The second time.

And she had time to get a little squinty-eyed before he couldn't hold out any longer.

Afterward he was quiet and disappointed.

"What is it?" she asked with her hand on the back of his neck.

"I want . . . I want it to . . . to be good . . . for you too," he mumbled.

"Silly," she said, just like the last time. "It's like I said—it never works the first time two people are together. You have to get to know each other. I did say that . . ."

Her words bit into him: It never works the first time two people are together.

Never.

How many guys had she been with to know this? To be able to say "never"?

It must be more than two. Four? Seven? Thirty?

A sharp-toothed rat started gnawing on his heart. Ai-ai-ai . . . He saw thirty guys standing in a row.

Ai-ai-ai, pain pain pain . . .

He almost got tears in his eyes before he remembered what else she'd said:

The first time.

It never works the first time, she'd said. And that was a promise that there would be a second time, and a third and . . . and many times.

Life is amazing.

"What are you thinking about?" she asked, laughing. "You look so happy."

"I'm thinking about a duck with red hair," he said, laughing, and kissed her on the nose.

They dozed off, intertwined between the wrinkled, sweaty sheets.

He couldn't remember having fallen asleep, but he woke up at dawn after just one hour of sleep. He raised himself up on his elbow and looked at the young woman who was sleeping on his pillow. She was lying on her side with her mouth open and one knee pulled up almost under her chin.

He was filled with a sense of calm and delight.

I've seen you sleep, he thought.

I've seen your red hair on my pillow, he thought.

I've seen your red hair sleeping on my pillow, he thought and drifted off to sleep again.

"You . . ."

She was whispering with her mouth against his ear.

"Wake up. Wake up, my handsome friend . . ."

He opened his eyes suddenly.

She was kneeling next to the bed, freshly showered and dressed.

"What is it?" he said sleepily. "What time is it? Where have you been?"

"In your bed," she said, smiling. "And it's seven-thirty. I have to get home before Mom comes home from work. So she doesn't have to worry. And I don't have to lie."

"Don't go," he mumbled. "Stay."

"I can't."

"When will we see each other then?" he said and sat up in bed. "Don't go . . ."

"I'm busy today," she said. "But tomorrow. Tomorrow, maybe?"

"No," he said sadly. "I'm going to the airport right after school gets out. Don't go . . ."

"Then we won't see each other until after America," she said. "Sad. But a month will go fast. Especially since it's summer vacation."

"A month is an eternity," he said. "I'll miss you every day. Every hour. Every minute. Every second. Don't go . . ."

She should have said: I'll miss you too. She didn't say that. She said:

"Oh, you'll meet so many cute American surfer girls that you'll have forgotten me after just a couple of days."

"There's no surfing on the East Coast. At least I don't think there is. And besides, I'll never forget you. Never in my life," he said, trying to hold her, to keep her there. "Don't go . . ."

She hugged him hard.

"I have to," she said and carefully twisted out of his arms.

In the doorway she turned and blew him a kiss.

"You can send me a postcard from America."

"I'll write you a long letter every day," he said. "Don't go . . ."

She blew him another kiss.

And left.

A frayed American flag

Now he's sitting with a frayed and worn American flag on his lap.

The star-spangled banner.

Wonder if the golf club in Marblehead got a new flag, he thought, grinning for the first time in a long time. They definitely needed to replace this old worn-out one anyway.

He had never put the flag up on his wall like he'd promised the Gang he would, and now he was going to get rid of it.

But how do you get rid of an American flag?

In the 60s demonstrators burned American flags and fought with the police, he'd seen pictures of it.

Maybe he should arrange his own little flag desecration ceremony, he thinks. A private little affair. Against American imperialism. His dad would certainly have approved.

No . . .

Nothing else will go up in flames tonight, he decides. Instead he gets his mom's sewing scissors and starts cutting.

After twenty minutes there isn't any of the proud star-spangled banner left in his room. Instead, lying on his desk, there are:

7 long red strips

6 long white strips

50 small blue squares with a white star on each.

"Goodbye," he says to himself and rakes all the bits of cloth into the wastebasket.

Stupid Susan, he thinks then. Stupid little Susan. And how stupid was I, he thinks, not to seize the opportunity. When I had an offer like that. If I had only known . . . Now it definitely hurts. Now he's crying again.

He cries and thinks a thought he's thought a thousand times before: If I hadn't gone to America, would nothing have happened then? Would everything have been all right then? Would everything have continued? Yes, he's thought that thought a thousand times: If I hadn't gone to America . . .

It's pointless to think that, but he can't help it. He thinks it again

    and cries

    and

    the phone

    sits

    silently

The letters to Heart's Delight

From the First Letter to Heart's Delight:

Everything here in America is so typical.

Everything here is exactly like it is in all the American movies and TV shows you see in Sweden. Or like in a Disney cartoon. The family I live with is named Brown, for example. Typical, huh? Mr. Brown works for an insurance company in Boston and earns lots of money, and Mrs. Brown has blue hair and a Martini shaker behind the breadbox in the kitchen. She chats and asks questions and is always so gushingly NICE, but she doesn't listen to my answers. That's typical for blue-haired American ladies, I think. But she's friendly.

Tom also lives here. The All-American Kid. He's fifteen years old and is supposed to be looking after me, but doesn't seem especially interested in having a Swedish guy follow him around all day. And I can understand that. I've met some of his friends. They seem very typical too. I still haven't met the sister: Jane, 19 years old. She lives up in New Hampshire with her boyfriend who's a Buddhist.

On the neatly manicured lawn in front of the house

there's a plastic flamingo and a family of ceramic deer, and every morning the paper boy bikes past and throws a rolled-up newspaper on the neatly raked walkway that leads to the front steps.

Everything is so typical . . .

I miss you. I've been here for two days. 26 days to go. It's like a punishment. Banishment.

I miss you.

From the Second Letter to Heart's Delight:

I haven't seen many black people here in Marblehead. Not even the garbagemen are black.

And down by the harbor, by the yacht club's clubhouse, which is like a giant wooden mansion, you only see white suntanned people. A black guy on the pier there would have stood out like a drunk in a midnight choir. (See, I know my Leonard Cohen too.) No, just white people and white sails. The Brown family has a big sailboat, of course, and we went out sailing on Sunday. It was some kind of competition, I think. I couldn't quite understand. We didn't win, at any rate. But Mrs. Brown had made a picnic lunch with five hundred triangular sandwiches out of white squishy bread wrapped up in Saran wrap:

"Do you want a tuna sandwich? Do you want a cheese

sandwich? Do you want a sandwich with tomatoes? Or with sliced ham? Or with egg? Or . . . ?" I ate four hundred sandwiches. And drank fifty cans of Coke.

In the evening there was a barbecue with the neighbors and Mr. Brown put on a special barbecuing outfit and grilled big steaks on the streamlined super-grill and all the neighbors were very curious about the exotic guest from Sweden and everyone asked questions and smiled and asked questions and smiled. But nobody listened when I answered. And nobody knew anything about Sweden or Europe. Sweden and Germany and Italy and Bulgaria are all the same to them. They think Europe is one big country. I think it's weird. They were well-educated, middle-class people. Any old ten-year-old in Sweden knows more about America than they know about Europe . . .

I miss you. I didn't know what the word MISS meant before. Now I know. 23 days left . . .

From the Fourth Letter to Heart's Delight:

I've seen another America now. The back side. Of course I knew before that there was something besides the wooden homes here in Marblehead, but now I've seen it with my own eyes.

Yesterday I went in to Boston with Mr. Brown.

Mrs. Brown was worried about me walking around alone in the big city, but Mr. Brown said that if I just stuck to downtown and didn't go to this or that part of town there wouldn't be any danger. As soon as he dropped me off on his way to work, I took a bus to one of the parts of town he'd warned me about.

When I hopped off the bus and rounded a street corner I almost crashed into an old black man who came staggering toward me, with his face all bloody. He said something in a slurred voice that I didn't understand and tried to grab ahold of me. I've never been so scared in all my life. And when I turned around to run away, I ran right into the arms of two sneering, black 19-year-olds who wanted cigarettes from me. I mumbled something about how I didn't smoke and managed to run past them and just then the bus came and I flung myself on it and went back downtown. I've never been so afraid in all my life. It still gives me shivers when I think about it.

It wasn't much better downtown. I saw junkies, prostitutes, beggars, old drunks, old women rummaging around in trash cans, and a gang of hoodlums. And of course there were a lot of shiny luxury businesses and palatial banks.

If Marblehead is a comedy or a family drama, then Boston is a detective story or a documentary.

But I didn't see anything that I hadn't already seen on TV . . .

Guess who I miss? Exactly. You. Miss miss miss miss you.

Yesterday I sat and wrote your name two thousand times on a piece of paper. It makes you stupid in the head, being in love. And I am . . .

From the Seventh Letter to Heart's Delight:

Do you remember that I wrote that everything here was so typical? That it feels like you've seen everything here on TV or at the movies already? Well, now I'm going to tell you the most typical thing of everything I've seen here: Tom's group of friends, the "gang."

The All-American Kid comes in four different types:

1. The charming troublemaker

2. The troublemaker who makes slightly too much trouble

3. The dumb, friendly, chubby kid

4. The skinny bookworm with thick glasses

And if you put a group of these four types together, you get the typical "gang" of American boys. The kind you've seen in thousands of movies and TV shows and read about in thousands of adventure stories. The GANG. When I met Tom's friends here I thought it was a joke at first. Tom himself is Type 1: A nice troublemaker, just the right mix of audacity and charm to get grownups to shake their heads and smile indulgently. His best friend's name is Steve (Type 2). Steve is a little too mischievous, a little too audacious, a little too daring, a little too wild, and the hero of the whole block. No grownups approve of Steve. But all the girls want to be with him. And many of them have been. (Tom will definitely turn out to be an insurance salesman like his dad. Or something else that's just as boring. But not Steve. He'll become some kind of crook, small-time gangster, huckster, vagabond, or millionaire. But he'll never put on a special barbecuing outfit!) Then we have Buzz (Type 3). Chubby Buzz who's always chewing on something, and sweating and huffing and puffing and whining any time he has to walk farther than a few blocks from the car to the nearest hamburgers. And finally there's Jeff (Type 4). He's pale and skinny and everyone thinks he's a genius. I don't know. He's good at doing math in his head, I'll give him that. He's totally a computer freak. And that's the Gang.

I had to laugh when I met them the first time. They were so stereotypical I thought it was a joke. But now I've gotten to know them and I kind of like them even if I'm not really one of the Gang but more like some kind of trainee.

The Gang meets every day and every day is pretty much

the same: We drive around in Steve's big Buick, we go to the beach, we swim or sail or go water-skiing (I learned how, it's not hard), and then we drive around some more and meet other gangs and cruise for girls (not me! not me!), the whole time with the car stereo blasting. And eat and eat and eat all the time, hamburgers and ice cream and pies and French fries and chocolate. Chew gum. Smoke Marlboros. And make plans for the weekend.

The weekend is a whole chapter of its own:

It starts on Friday afternoons with Buzz sneaking off with some money for Miss Lewis. She's this half-crazed old lady who walks around in a thick winter coat the whole summer. And an alcoholic. Two hours later Buzz sneaks over to Miss Lewis again and comes back with three brown paper bags that clink. In the bags there are a few bottles of strong, sweet alcoholic cider and some six-packs of beer. The guys are deathly afraid that their parents will find out that they drink, so they drive miles and miles away on Friday night before they dare to start drinking. And then we end up in some deserted cemetery or vacant lot somewhere, and then we drink and make a bunch of noise and fight (not me) and make out with girls (not me! not me!) and sometimes other gangs chase us and sometimes we chase other gangs and once this angry farmer came and shot at us with a shotgun. He looked like Elmer Fudd and we ran for our lives.

And Jeff throws up and Buzz falls asleep in a bush.

Then someone looks at the clock and realizes it's high time we went home, and then, as if by magic, everyone kind of sobers up and smooths out their clothing and starts looking for Buzz and brushing themselves off and popping mints. Then we drive home and slip into bed.

The same program every Friday night. Rerun again on Saturday. On Monday everyone talks about how the weekend was, tries to sort out what happened and what everyone did, and on Tuesday everyone starts planning for the next weekend . . .

Only ten days left . . .

From the Ninth Letter to Heart's Delight:

I haven't thought about holes in the ozone a single time during these weeks. Or about hunger or injustice in the world. Or overpopulation. Or acid rain. Or nuclear weapons. Or the future. Those are things I always used to think about.

I've only thought of you.

It's lucky that all people don't fall in love at the same

time. That there are some people who have other things on their minds. Or maybe it's too bad it's that way . . .

From the Twelfth Letter to Heart's Delight:

Tonight there's a full moon. Which makes me think of you. Do you know why? Yes, of course you know. My whole life I will always think of you when I see a full moon, I promise. And I will always see you standing in my room and showing me the full moon and explaining what the full moon means for you.

I see that image like a painting in front of me.

Tomorrow I'm flying over the Atlantic. Home. I'll be home before this letter, but I couldn't help writing it anyway. By the time this letter reaches Sweden, I will already have been with you. It's almost inconceivable.

Hugs and hugs and hugs and hugs

He wrote twelve letters to Heart's Delight. He wrote twelve long letters and received one single postcard in response:

Hi!

Read your third letter on the beach today. It's so hot here that you have to be down near the water so you don't pass out. I'm living off ice cream and sunshine. I'll be tan

and fat when we see each other again. Come home soon!
(We need to talk)
    Ann-Katrin

That was it.

And still: When he read "Come home soon!" he was almost ready to cut his America-stay short and fly home to Sweden.

"Come home soon!"

Maybe it was a cry for help. Or a desperate prayer. Or a threat: If you don't come home soon, then . . .

He didn't think about (We need to talk) that much. He didn't understand (We need to talk) until he came home.

Yup, he wrote twelve letters in four weeks.

Still, he didn't say everything.

He didn't say anything about the sheet. That he fell asleep every night with a used sheet in his arms. The sheet that he and she had lain on, he'd brought it with him, and every night he lay there and sniffed it and snuggled with it. Like a one-year-old with a security blanket or a teddy bear.

Every morning he hid the sheet in his suitcase again.

He also didn't say anything about how one calm evening, while it was still light out, he and Steve sat in a little boat on a lake and smoked three marijuana cigarettes. He coughed and giggled.

"Where'd you get them from?" he asked, nodding toward the cigarettes.

"Dad's got a secret box. Hidden in a secret place." Steve grinned. "I took them from there. Pass the joint."

"Does your dad smoke this?" he asked, surprised.

"Everybody does," Steve responded, shrugging his shoulders.

But that wasn't really true, because Tom and the other guys didn't smoke marijuana.

"Never," said Tom. "No way."

Everyone, even Steve, agreed that alcohol was more fun than marijuana.

Everyone agreed that drugs were dangerous.

Everyone also agreed that marijuana wasn't a drug. Not a real drug.

The third thing he didn't say anything about in his letters was Susan. Cute, freckled Susan, who'd been Steve's girlfriend for a while a long time ago. And many other guys' girlfriend too, according to Tom.

Even on the first Saturday night he'd ended up with her in a junkyard. They each sat on a pile of tires with a bottle of cider between them while the rest of the Gang ran around and shouted in between the wrecked cars.

"Have you got a girlfriend back in Sweden?" Susan asked him, taking a swig of cider.

He nodded.

"Can't I make you forget her? Just for tonight?" Susan asked. She leaned toward him.

"No. I'm sorry." He smiled and patted her cheek.

He'd been vaccinated against smallpox and girls before he came to America. The girl vaccine was Heart's Delight.

He just plain wasn't interested. Maybe that was why Susan, and some other girls too, found him interesting.

No, he didn't say anything about Susan in his letters. Which is why he couldn't tell her how it happened that he got an American flag as a going-away present from the Gang.

His last night in Marblehead the Brown family organized a little party for him, and late that night, when the coals had died down in the grill and the Coca-Cola was all drunk up, Tom came and grabbed hold of his arm.

"Hey, Swede, we've got a little surprise for you," he whispered secretively.

Tom pulled him along, up into the attic. It was completely pitch black up there, but suddenly someone turned on the light and he saw Susan standing in the middle of the floor wrapped in an American flag.

Four rough, cracking teenage voices began to sing:

"Oh say can you see by the dawn's early light . . ."

It was Jeff and Buzz and Steve who were hiding up

there, and together with Tom they sang the whole national anthem for him:

"... the land of the free and the home of the brave."

The whole time, Susan stood there silent, smiling flirtatiously and swaying her hips in time with the song.

When the guys finished singing, Tom said, "It's for you: Unwrap her!"

He went up to Susan.

"Have you got any clothes on under there?" he asked.

"You'll find out soon enough," she answered, handing him the edge of the flag.

When he took hold of the flag, she elegantly spun herself out of it.

No, she wasn't naked. She was wearing a small, pointy black bra and a black G-string.

Buzz whistled, Tom licked his lips, and Jeff looked upward as if he were thanking God.

But Susan didn't seem to notice anyone but him. She looked him straight in the eyes and then threw her arms around his neck and pressed her freckled body against his.

"It's not too late yet," she whispered and stuck her tongue in his ear.

She smelled like cider.

"Yes it is." He smiled and pushed her away. "I'm sorry." Then he turned toward the Gang. "Thanks, boys.

I'll put it on my wall. In my room. In Sweden. Thank you. I'll look at it and remember you."

"Yeah," said Steve. "But don't show it to anybody here. We stole it down by the clubhouse. By the golf course. They'll miss it tomorrow."

No, despite his twelve letters to Heart's Delight, there were still some things he hadn't told her about:

A sheet.

Three cigarettes.

Freckled Susan.

And a flag ceremony.

A black notebook

A black notebook with a red spine and red corners. A cheap notebook made in China that he bought at Konsum before he left for America.

He reads it. He wrote what he's reading.

She came in from the fog
Her red hair
Lit up my morning
Lit up my life

He counts on his fingers. Eight. Eight months ago.
Only eight months.
He sighs deeply and flips through the notebook.

The tea tasted like tea
The bread tasted like bread
The jam tasted like jam
My woman tasted like lemon

Actually it was scones, he thinks. Not bread. He sighs again before he continues reading.

I've seen you sleep
Who saw? I did
Who did I see? You
What were you doing? Sleeping
I was awake
you slept
and I saw you

There were two versions of the next one. First he'd written:

I have been in you
Now you are in me

After that he wrote:

I have been in you
two times
Now you are in me
forever

He stretches in the chair and thinks: No!

He shuts his eyes and thinks: No!

He thinks "No!" for four minutes before he turns the page in the notebook and reads on.

When I fall asleep in my bed
you are there
When I wake the next day
you are there

You are always there
—but never here
And here is not there

When I'm in a car
when I'm in a boat
when I read my book
when I dream my dream
when I eat my food
when I wash my plate
you are there
And one day there will be here

On the next page he starts reading:

You open doors
for me
You show me worlds
I didn't know existed
When you open yourself to me
you open doors
in my hea—

He slams the book shut with a bang.

Now he thinks painful thoughts, now he sees painful images, now he sees how they're reading together, no, of course, she's reading and translating and they're giggling together and . . .

He hits the book hard, with a clenched fist.

Ahh.

Damned Duck, he thinks.

Damned Nazi, he thinks.

And tears out all the notebook pages he had written on, and tears the pages into small pieces of confetti, and rushes into the bathroom and flushes the pieces, and flushes and flushes long after all the pieces have disappeared down into the sewer.

He does all this as if in a rage, but then the air goes

out of him and he stands there for a long time, bent over the toilet.

Is the phone sitting silently in his room?

Yes.

Heart's Delight on the other side of the Atlantic

No, he didn't just write letters in America. He also wrote poems in his black Chinese notebook.

Poems? Well . . . Maybe notes. Thoughts. Or journal entries. It was a kind of diary. The truth was that he often felt like he was only half present during his month in America.

Just 30–40% sometimes.

And just 5% when he fell asleep with his sheet against his cheek.

The rest of him, the part that wasn't in Marblehead, Massachusetts, was with Heart's Delight on the other side of the Atlantic. And he was forced to write, it was the only thing he could do with his longing.

Write to her, about her, about himself and all the new unknowns that were bubbling up in him at dawn each day and that kept him awake until late into the night.

She gave him no peace. Her power stretched over the ocean.

In his letters to her he wasn't always entirely honest.

Or rather: He did not give a truly accurate picture of Marblehead, Massachusetts, U.S.A. Nor did he give a truly accurate picture of himself there.

Everything wasn't that typical at all.

Mrs. Brown certainly didn't have blue hair.

Steve didn't have a Buick. (Jeff's older brother, on the other hand, had a rusty Opel.)

And there was no Gang. Well, sure, there was a gang, but the boys were not movie stereotypes like he had described them. As a matter of fact, he thought they were a little too childish for him, and they thought he was a bit of a fuddy-duddy. Thus he wasn't especially interested in spending time with them and they weren't especially interested in having him along, so when the Gang was out driving around (in the Opel) or swimming, he was often sitting at home in the shade in the yard next to the flamingo

and reading

and writing

and dreaming

and longing.

No, he wasn't entirely honest in his letters. But in his poems-notes-thoughts he was. More honest than he'd ever been, he thought.

And everything he wrote in his black notebook, he also sent to her. He just couldn't not send them. They were messages directly from his heart. To hers. He was sure of it.

It was simply inconceivable that anyone else would ever read what he'd written to her. That thought was impossible. There wasn't even a 0.05% chance that it could happen. Or a risk.

And he wrote directly from his heart to Heart's Delight on the other side of the Atlantic.

A package with a curly ribbon

An exquisite package with shiny paper and a curly ribbon. Just the kind of package you would want to get on your birthday, or discover sitting under the Christmas tree and shake a little bit and squeeze a little bit . . .

An exquisite package.

Still, he doesn't look happy sitting there with the package in front of him on his desk, and he doesn't squeeze the package curiously and he doesn't shake it.

No, he doesn't look happy at all. He looks unhappy. And he is not curious, because he knows what's in the package. He bought it himself. He bought it in America to give to Heart's Delight when he came home. He searched for a present for a long time, one that would be good enough, nice enough. And when he had finally found the thing that is in the package in front of him, he had been satisfied.

Why hadn't she gotten it, then? He had had it with him when he rushed over to see her early the first morning after he got home. The package had sat on her kitchen table.

Why hadn't she gotten it? Why was it sitting on his desk now, still unopened?

Now she'll never get it, and now he wants to get rid of it. He takes it with him out into the stairwell, but he doesn't walk down the hall to the garbage chute; he goes up one floor instead. It says R. Persson on the door that he sets the package down in front of. He rings the doorbell twice, quickly, and races down the stairs again. But he doesn't close the door to the apartment. He stands still and listens with the door ajar and hears Rune Persson open his door on the floor above.

"What? What the hell? Hello! What . . . what's this? What the hell?" Rune grunts and can be heard lifting the package up and shaking it. He isn't exactly sober, that can be heard too.

"Hrm. What the hell?" Rune mumbles and stands in the doorway for a second, but when no one steps out and yells "Surprise!" he goes back into his apartment and closes the door behind him. He takes the package with him.

So, the package finally ended up with Rune Persson. Will a lonely old man be happy to get a bracelet, authentic Indian craftsmanship, and a thick book in English, *The Complete Leonard Cohen*?

The phone sits silently. The only sound that can be heard in the apartment is that of someone crying, quietly and for a long time.

Heart's Delight and him and him

No. It won't do to cut this scene either. What kind of film would it be then? This is no gushy, sentimental, happy teenage love story. Or some trashy romantic B-movie.

This isn't *Grease* or *The Blue Lagoon*. This is pure, stark realism. The audience will cry. And the audience is just him, and of course he cries his way through the final showing, but this specific scene makes him blush first.

How could he be so dumb and so blind?

He is ashamed and flushed and astounded at his own stupidity, at least in the beginning. Then it starts to hurt. The kind of pain that can come only from having a sharp-toothed rat gnawing on your heart.

Heart's Delight, scene 12
Location: Her apartment
Time: Early in the morning
Starring:
HIM played by himself
HEART'S DELIGHT played by Ann-Katrin
NAZI-HANS played by Hans-Peter Switzerland Guy

(What? Why three parts? Why not just two? This is, after all, the first time they'll see each other after his America trip, and he had hurried over to see her with his exquisite package first thing in the morning even though he didn't get home from the airport until late the night before. Why three parts?)

Shh! Quiet!
We're starting! Roll camera!
TAKE ONE!

He comes running up the
stairs, stops in front of her
door, catches his breath for a
second, then rings the
doorbell; when no one opens
after five seconds he rings
one more time impatiently,
and one more time. Then
the door opens.

HEART'S DELIGHT:
(still half asleep, wearing
her bathrobe)
What? Is it you? I
thought . . .

HIM:
(happily) Hi! Good
morning, sleepyhead!
Remember me?

He wants to hug her, he pulls
her toward him, she lets herself
be hugged but seems more
surprised than happy. After a
little bit she pushes him away.

HEART'S DELIGHT:
I thought . . . I thought you
weren't coming until
tomorrow.

He wants to go in. She is still
standing in the doorway.

You did write . . . that you
would come tomorrow
night . . . right?

HIM:
Mmm, the plan was to
stay in New York for
three days at the end. But
it got cut short.

He laughs.

You seem nervous. Have you got a secret lover hidden in your closet or something?

She doesn't laugh, but puts her hand on his shoulder.

HEART'S DELIGHT: Come in for a bit. I haven't had breakfast yet. Come on.

He follows her into the apartment and sits down at the kitchen table while she gets out some food for breakfast and puts water on to make tea. He sets the package next to him on the kitchen table. He sits silently. She is also silent while she sets the table for breakfast. Finally she sets cups of tea for each of them on the table and sits down directly across from him.

HEART'S DELIGHT:
So . . .

They both lift their teacups,
blow on the hot tea, and
drink carefully. Silence.
Then they look up.

HIM & HEART'S
DELIGHT:
(at the same time)
You/Did . . .

They both giggle.

HIM:
What were you going
to say?

HEART'S DELIGHT:
No, you start.

HIM:
Did . . . did you get my
letters?

HEART'S DELIGHT:
Mmm. Yeah. Thank you.
I had stuff to read on the

beach almost every single day. It's been totally hot here, I . . .

HIM:
(interrupts her) How many letters did you get?

HEART'S DELIGHT:
Lots.

HIM:
I wrote twelve.

HEART'S DELIGHT:
(laughs) Then there are probably still some on the way . . .

It gets quiet again. She gets up and goes to the sink; he follows her, stands behind her, and tries to undo the belt of her robe.

HEART'S DELIGHT:
No, cut it out, wait . . .

He takes a step back.

HIM:
What is it? Has something happened? I . . . What is it?

She turns to face him and puts her hand on his cheek.

HEART'S DELIGHT:
You . . . We need to talk. You and me. Come and sit down . . .

He holds her hand against his cheek and kisses her fingertips, one by one.

HIM:
Mmm . . . You taste good. Still. Just as good as I . . . you . . . I . . .

He takes a deep breath.

I've . . . missed you . . . the whole time . . .

She pulls her hand back.

HEART'S DELIGHT:
There's something you don't know yet. I have a—

NAZI-HANS:
Guten Morgen!

He's startled. Out of her room comes a tan, broad-shouldered, short-haired young man wearing an unbuttoned short-sleeved shirt. The young man is buttoning his pants as he enters the kitchen and flashes a big white-toothed smile.

HEART'S DELIGHT:
—visitor. This is Hans-Peter. I met him on a ski trip last winter. When Lotta and I were in Switzerland. And now he and his friend hitchhiked here to see us. I'm sure I told you I was going to have a guest, that Hans-Peter was coming?

HIM:
(gaping, speechless)
Uh . . . ?

NAZI-HANS:
(smiles, extends his hand)
Guten Morgen. Servus.
Hallo.

He hesitantly takes the hand
being extended toward him.
Nazi-Hans shakes it
energetically.

HIM:
Uh . . . Hi . . .

HEART'S DELIGHT:
They're leaving tomorrow.
They're going on to
Stockholm, then over to
Finland, and then . . .

He looks at her in
astonishment.

What's wrong . . . ?

When he doesn't respond
she turns away and

CUT!
That'll do, thanks. Good.

Yes, that's how it was. And what makes him blush when
he sees this scene is that he didn't understand.

He thought it was annoying that she wasn't home alone,
that he didn't get to be alone with her and tell her about
America and explain things he'd written in his letters, and she
would be curious and ask lots of questions, and then he would
give her the package and . . . and tell her how much he'd
missed her and . . . and touch her, of course. Make love to her.

He couldn't do any of that since he was not alone with
her. But he didn't get any tears in his eyes, not tears of
anger, not tears of sadness.

He didn't even feel jealous.

He just thought: Oh, she has a friend visiting. Oh. Well,
if she says so, then it must be so. What a shame. But there's
no helping it. At least he's leaving tomorrow.

Yup, it's true. That's how dumb he was.

It's actually true.

And there they sat at her kitchen table, Heart's Delight
and him and him.

"Blablablabla," he said, "bla blabla."

"Blablabla blabla," said Heart's Delight.

"Wunderbutten wunderbutten," said Nazi-Hans. "Wunderbutten."

"Wunderbutten," Heart's Delight responded. "Wunderbutten wienerschnitzel . . ."

"Bla blabla blabla," he said.

And so on.

He didn't once think of Nazi-Hans as Nazi-Hans. He called Nazi-Hans "Hans-Peter," pleasantly and courteously. He didn't understand.

He didn't wonder where Nazi-Hans had slept, and if he had, then he would have thought: On a mattress on the floor, of course, or in a sleeping bag on a Therm-a-Rest. Of course. Obviously. He couldn't even think of anything else.

It sounds unbelievable, but it's true.

"Couldn't . . . Couldn't we get together later today, or tonight maybe?" he tried after a while.

"We're going to the movies tonight," she answered. "Lotta and Jurgen and . . . well, Hans-Peter and I. Then they're leaving tomorrow. So then we could . . ."

"Are you going to the seven or the nine o'clock show? I'll come along to the movie, that might be fun. If that's okay . . . ?" he said, laughing as if he'd said something funny.

She wasn't smiling.

Something had happened to her smile, but he didn't notice that either.

"Sure, of course you could," she said after a while, shrugging her shoulders.

Then she smiled a little bit at least:

"Of course you can come along. Sure. Why don't you meet us in front of Scala then. At eight-thirty."

He nodded, pleased.

"Good. Cool," he said.

Then it got quiet around the table.

She started clearing the table and Nazi-Hans sat and smiled his dazzling white smile. No one said anything.

Finally he stood up.

"I'm going to go home and sleep for a bit then," he said. "Eight hours on the plane. And I got home at two in the morning. And there's the time difference. I'm beat. Actually."

He didn't know then how beat he was.

"Eight-thirty tonight then?"

"Yes." She nodded and glanced curiously at the package that he took with him on his way out. He noticed her glance but didn't say anything. He didn't want to leave it now, it could wait until tomorrow. Giving someone a present was more of a two-person thing.

"Bye," she said, trying to make her voice sound intimate. She leaned forward and gave him a kiss on the cheek.

"Bye. See you tonight."

He sensed a little smile. And the hint of that little smile kept him from noticing that the kiss had been an okay-then-why-don't-you-get-going kiss.

A movie ticket

A used movie ticket stub. A nine o'clock show at Scala. He folds it and blows on it, getting it to make a loud noise the way he and his friends used to do with blades of grass. Oh . . . It echoes in the empty apartment. Oh.

He smiles a little to himself and is filled for a few moments by old memories of hanging out with friends. The ten-year-old memories make him warm for a brief while until he remembers . . . that the movie he's watching tonight is called *Heart's Delight*.

The childhood happiness quickly drains out of him. He looks at the ticket again. How was the movie? Good or bad? Boring or funny? Interesting or meaningless? Exciting or beautiful or . . . ?

He doesn't know. He doesn't remember. He was there, he sat there, but he still didn't watch the movie.

From his theater visit he remembers only the strange feeling of sitting next to Heart's Delight and still feeling like she was just as far away as when he was in America. It was an awful feeling.

Brrr. He shudders when he thinks about it.

And then. On the way home . . .

Doesn't this movie ever end?

A used movie ticket stub can't be hard to get rid of. On his bookshelf there's a pile of library books. He stuffs the ticket stub into the thinnest book, behind the checkout card in the very back of the book.

Tomorrow he'll go to the library. Or maybe someone else will return his books . . .

He puts the book back on the shelf. *The Sorrows of Young Werther* by J. W. von Goethe. He sets it next to the phone, which sits silently.

Former Heart's Delight

By eight o'clock he was standing outside Scala waiting. He was impatient.

He'd been lying in his bed since visiting her that morning, but he had not been able to sleep for a single minute even though he was dead tired.

His body was dead tired, but his heart was wide awake. Pounding and wide awake.

Now he was walking restlessly back and forth outside the theater. After he looked in some store windows to the left of Scala he went back and looked in some store windows to the right of the theater, the whole time keeping an eye on the theater entrance. He would not have been able to list a single thing that was in any of the windows to the right or left of Scala. He would not even have been able to tell you what kind of stores they were. If someone were to ask, that is.

It was quarter to by the time they arrived. He saw them when they were still quite a way away. They were happy and talking; both the Swiss guys were gesticulating and waving their arms, and the two girls were laughing. He walked up to them.

"Hi . . . Hello there. Hi!"

The laughing and talking stopped.

"Hi," Lotta said.

He recognized her from the bus. Now she gave him a friendly smile, and after she'd studied him for a moment, she said:

"Hi. I'm Lotta. Ann-Ka has told me about you. I think I've seen you on the bus."

"Mmm," he said, nodding.

"And this is Jurgen," Lotta continued. "From Switzerland."

"Hallo," Jurgen said, nodding. "Servus."

"Hallo," said Nazi-Hans.

Jurgen and Nazi-Hans were just like twins. But Jurgen had dark hair. They could both have moonlighted for some company that sold outdoor equipment and sporting gear:

"Jurgen, on the left, is wearing a wind-resistant cotton jacket with removable fleece lining in crimson ($149) and a pair of expedition pants in reinforced, waterproof canvas ($98), while Hans-Peter, on the right . . ."

Yes, in front of him stood two clean, healthy Europeans.

"Hi, Switzerland," he said again, thinking he was funny. Heart's Delight slowly shook her head and came over to him.

"Hi," she said, putting her hand on his upper arm.

"Come on, let's go in. Did you buy your ticket already? We've been out to eat, at an Italian restaurant, that's why we're a little late. It was great. Come on."

What? Why hadn't she said that they were going to go out to eat? Why hadn't he gotten to go along? Why . . . ?

But her hand on his arm silenced his unvoiced questions, and he felt a warm surge run through him. Everything was good. He suddenly felt entirely at peace.

Everything was good.

She and Lotta wanted to eat with the Swiss guys before they left. A goodbye dinner. Completely natural.

He was a hundred percent confident. He was a hundred percent stupid too, but he didn't know that.

But in the movie theater his uneasiness returned again.

She was sitting next to him, just a few inches to the left of him, and still she was infinitely far away. He wanted to talk to her, touch her, caress her, feel her, smell her, taste her. But he couldn't do anything. His hand looked for hers in the darkness of the movie theater.

"Not now," she whispered, putting his hand back on his own knee, "not now."

No, he didn't see the movie.

When the light came on in the movie theater and people started to get up and push their way toward the exits he looked around in confusion, blinking his eyes as if he'd been asleep. Was it over? Was the movie over already?

"Come on now, there's not going to be any more." Heart's Delight laughed and pulled him up. "There won't be any more. It's over. The end. Finito."

They walked home together. He pushed his bike. If he hadn't had his bicycle to drag along, he would have been able to put his arm around her. He needed that. Now he could only walk near her and try to press up against her now and then. But she didn't press back.

"What did you think?" Lotta asked. "About the movie, I mean?"

"Oh . . ." he said dumbly. "Uh . . ."

"Well, that was an exhaustive analysis," said Lotta, laughing. "That's precisely what I thought. Exactly."

He shot Lotta an appreciative glance. She was fun.

"Uh . . . I kind of fell asleep," he said. "I'm . . . I'm completely beat. After my trip . . ."

No, that wasn't true.

He hadn't slept, he'd been awake. But still he hadn't seen the movie.

That he was beat, however, that was true. But he didn't know that yet.

He would discover it in a moment.

"Here's where we turn off," Lotta said at a street corner. "We're heading home now. Bye!"

"Gute Nacht," Jurgen said and waved.

"See you tomorrow morning, early," said Lotta to Heart's Delight.

"Have a nice time," Heart's Delight said, smiling knowingly.

Yes. Lotta and Jurgen went on their way. They held on to each other, laughed and kissed each other. They practically glowed with lust.

He peered after them, nodding to himself. Yes, they would certainly have a nice time.

It was then that he turned toward her, toward Heart's Delight. It was then that he saw her glance. Her glance and her smile toward Nazi-Hans.

They had been standing and watching as Lotta and Jurgen walked away. Now they were looking at each other . . .

He recognized that smile. Mona Lisa. He knew what it meant.

Only then did it dawn on him.

That's how long it took him to understand.

Not until then did he understand that he was out. That he was finished. That he was history.

Sidelined. Shut out. Through.

Only then did he see that he'd been blind.

A chasm opened before him. He was suddenly cold, he shivered, he was sweating, sharp teeth started munching at his heart, a hard heavy lump grew inside him, his eyes filled with tears, he wanted to cry, he wanted to punch something, he wanted . . . he wanted nothing, he wanted to die.

"Well, we should also . . ." Heart's Delight began, but then she noticed him there, standing bent over his bike with his head down. "What is it? Are you sick? Aren't you feeling well? You . . . you look really pale!"

She came over to him, she wanted to support him, help him, but he twisted away from her.

"Leave me alone!"

She looked at him in surprise.

He turned away.

She, who was no longer Heart's Delight but had, in a few seconds, transformed into a complete stranger, looked at him.

Did she understand that he understood? No, not really, not yet. The former Heart's Delight looked at him in astonishment.

There are several different versions of what happened next. This scene had been changed in each showing of the movie-in-his-head. Here are some examples:

VERSION 1

He glanced up and looked at her through a veil of tears.

"It's not fair," he said, trying to keep the emotion out of his voice. "It's not fair."

"What isn't?" she said uneasily. "What isn't?"

"I missed you . . . so much. The whole time I was missing you. And longing for you. It's not fair."

She stood silently.

"I've never been in love . . . never been so in love . . . as with you. You must feel something for me. Otherwise it's just not fair . . ."

She stood silently and stared at the ground. Nazi-Hans stood just behind her. He understood nothing.

VERSION 2

He glanced up and looked her squarely in the eyes.

"Where is he sleeping?"

"What?" she said.

She said that to win herself a little time.

"Where is he sleeping? Him. Nazi-Hans," he said and nodded.

"His name is Hans-Peter," she said tersely. "And where he's sleeping is none of your business."

He nodded bitterly to himself.

"Heil Hitler," he said and did a stern Nazi salute toward

the startled Nazi-Hans. Have a nice time. Then he took his bike and left.

VERSION 3

He glanced up and looked at her scornfully.

"Is he good?"

"What?" she said. "What do you mean?"

"Is he good? In bed, I mean. In your bed," he said coldly. "Is he a good fuck?"

She turned away from him.

"Come on, we're leaving," she said and took Nazi-Hans's arm. "Wir gehen nach Hause."

"Is he better than me?" he shouted in desperation after them. Then she turned and walked up to him.

"I don't compare guys," she said, staring him squarely in the eyes, "and I don't fuck. I make love. And only with guys I really like a lot."

"And how many guys can you really like a lot at the same time?" he asked. "Two, three, four, seven? Or some whole sports team. Or, shit . . ."

He quieted down and stared at the ground.

"You don't own me," she said.

After a moment of silence she continued in a softer voice: "I'll see you tomorrow. We can talk then."

"Over my dead body," he said and bicycled away.

VERSION 4

He glanced up and saw that she also had tears in her eyes. Even though he hadn't said anything, she understood. He understood that she had understood.

"You," she said with sadness in her voice, "you . . . Everything is going wrong today. It was never supposed to be like this. You . . ."

She moved right up next to him and looked at him pleadingly. He bit his lip and stood silently.

"You," she continued, "I missed you too, those first days after you left I thought only of you, and then, as things started getting back to normal, Hans-Peter came and his visit had been planned for such a long time, and . . . You . . . We could definitely try . . . I've never felt the way I did with you. You . . ."

He bit his lip so hard that it almost started bleeding, but said nothing, just turned away, took his bike, and left.

VERSION 5

He glanced up and without a word went over to Nazi-Hans.

"Take this, Nazi pig," he said and gave him a hard kick between the legs.

Nazi-Hans doubled over in pain and fell down slowly, as if in slow motion, onto the street.

He cast a cold glance down at Nazi-Hans where he lay hunched up and whimpering.

"You won't get much use out of him tonight," he said, turning toward her, "you horny bitch . . ."

Stop!

Surely that last version is way too far from reality to be of any interest?

Reality, right. What really happened?

Something like this:

VERSION 0

He glanced up and looked at her.

Was it really possible? He started to feel sick. His legs didn't want to hold him up.

"I have to go home," he said feebly. "I don't feel good."

She looked at him attentively and seriously. Now she understood that he had understood.

"You," she said, "go home and sleep now. I'll call you tomorrow. We have to talk."

"I don't want to," he whispered helplessly.

"What?" she said leaning toward him. "What?"

He didn't say anything else, just turned away, jumped up onto his bike, and rode away.

How he got home that evening he couldn't remember.
That's about how it went.
But version 1
        version 2
        version 3
        and
        version 4
were not completely wrong either.

A razor blade and a bottle of pills

The question wasn't "if." Or "why." The question was "how."

To be or not to be? Not to be. But how?

How do you take your own life?

How do you do yourself in?

How do you call it quits?

How do you die?

1. Pistol.

   Classic, quick, probably almost pain-free. But how do you get hold of a pistol? If you don't know someone who belongs to a gun club. Or who's a terrorist.

2. Jump from a great height.

   No way! He didn't even have the courage to jump off the high board at the swimming pool. And the fear on the way down. And what if you changed your mind then . . . ?!

3. Drowning.

   Hard. If you're a good swimmer. And horrible: to feel the panic, not to be able to fight it . . .

4. Hanging.

   Also classic. But also hard: where do you attach the rope? And painful. Way too painful.

5. Throw yourself in front of a train.

   No. Don't mix some innocent railway engineer up in this. No.

6. Gassing.

   Maybe good. But where? He didn't know anyone with a gas stove.

7. Burn yourself up.

   Never. That would be the last thing he would do. That would never be the last thing he would do.

Yes, how was hard.

But he has had two other alternatives on his list, and now he sits at his desk with a razor blade in his hand. He places it carefully against his left wrist where he can feel his blood pulsing. Just a quick cut and then the blood would pump out, spurt by spurt it would pump out of his body, out into his room. NO!

No! No! Not like that either!

He couldn't do it.

And he doesn't want his mom to come home and see him in a pool of blood. And imagine if it were Hanna who came into his room first. A small, innocent child.

She would have nightmares for the rest of her life.

No! No!

He hurries out to the bathroom and puts the razor blade back in Krister's Gillette package.

Brrr . . . His horrible thoughts make him shiver and shake.

Then all that remains is:

9. A bottle of pills.

He picks up the bottle and contemplates it:

VALIUM. 50 pills. 10 mg. Blue pills. He looked up in mom's *PDR* and saw that the blue ones are the strongest. Good. And the bottle is almost full. Mom must have gotten them to comfort her after one of her crises, maybe her thirtieth birthday crisis or her fortieth birthday crisis or her divorce or whatever, but she'd taken only a couple of pills. Good. Yes. It'll be pills. That's clean and quick and simple. A handful of pills, a few glasses of water, and then fall asleep. That's what it'll be.

Then it's just a matter of not throwing them up.

Yes. It'll be pills.

He leans back in the chair. When the movie is over, it'll be pills, he thinks.

But she still has a chance to prevent it. She still has power over his life. And over his death. But not much longer, he thinks and stares at the silent phone.

Life after Heart's Delight

When he came home the night they went to the movies he had chills and crawled into bed right away. The whole night he lay there tossing and turning in despair, alternately burning up and freezing cold, and the new day had already dawned by the time he finally fell asleep.

After a few hours' sleep he woke up, and for five seconds, maybe ten, he felt good. He felt thoroughly refreshed and good, and sat up in bed.

Then he remembered what had happened and fell backward onto the bed. And fell and fell and fell and fell. Through all the painful memories from yesterday that had already started crowding into his head, he heard the phone ring, he heard his mom answer and talk to someone, and then her voice when she opened his door a crack:

"Hello! Are you awake? The phone's for you. It's Ann-Kat . . ."

He pretended to be asleep and tried to breathe calmly and deeply as if he were asleep to trick his mom.

She sighed and went back to the phone. Now he listened and heard her say:

"No, he's still asleep, I'm sure he's tired after his trip and the time change, jet lag you know, should I have him call you when he wakes up? . . . Uh-huh . . . All right, good. Bye!"

He stayed in bed all day.

"Are you sick?" his mom asked.

"I think I have a little bit of a fever," he replied.

"Ann-Katrin called this morning," his mom said. "She'll call again."

"Mmm."

The phone rang twice that day and both times he flung himself at it to get to the receiver before his mom answered. The first time the phone rang he picked up the receiver without saying anything and heard her voice:

"Hello? Is that . . ."

He quickly shoved the receiver under his pillow and pressed down. Hard. And for a long time.

He sat tight for ten minutes before he picked up the pillow. The phone call had long since been suffocated by then, of course.

The second time he pulled the cord out of the jack as soon as he heard the ring.

He was sure that it was her. And he didn't want to talk to her.

He never wanted to talk to her again.

The rest of the day was spent crying.

And suffering.

And thinking through everything that happened the day before, from his standing with his nice package outside her door early in the morning, until he biked home through the night with tears of despair in his eyes . . .

And tormenting himself with images: Every single frame of the movie was a knife in his heart.

And every time he played the scenes for himself he discovered details that he hadn't noticed yesterday.

For example, now he saw

her expression when she opened the door to him in the morning: She looked as happy as if it were Jehovah's Witnesses or someone conducting a survey who was standing outside her door.

Why is the little jerk here now, a day too early? she'd thought. Why is the little shrimp here bugging me now when super-cute Hans-Peter Naziman with hair on his chest is here visiting? she'd thought.

Yes. That's what she'd thought.

And now, for example, he saw

how she mentioned his letters but didn't even know how many she'd received. She probably hadn't even opened them. Or she'd read them aloud at the beach to Lotta and the Switzer-nuts, and giggled and made fun of his stupid poems, and then left the opened letters lying around on the beach so that anyone could read them.

In fact, hadn't she herself given him Björn's postcard? Suddenly he felt a strong feeling of solidarity with Björn. Whoever he might be . . .

And, for example, he saw

how Nazi-Hans came out of her bedroom. Now he knew where Nazi had slept, and he saw over and over again in detail how Nazi came out of her bedroom, buttoning his pants

and buttoning his pants

and buttoning his pants,

and now the Green-Eyed Monster started to show him terror-pornography:

Her hands when she unbuttoned his pants. When she pulled down his pants. Her hands on his body. His hands on her body. Her lips . . . Her tongue . . . Their naked bodies . . .

AAAAAAAAAAAAHHHHHHH!!!!!

"What is it? What is it?"

Mom stood in the doorway.

"What is it?" she asked anxiously. "You screamed and . . ."

"I was dreaming," he said, breathing heavily. "Such a terrible nightmare."

The nightmare tormented him all day. And all the next day. And the next and the next and the next.

It surfaced at regular intervals, he couldn't defend himself against it, he couldn't press the OFF button, and it was unbearably painful.

At the same time he kept replaying that last day's scenes over and over again, and still each time he watched the movie-in-his-head he found new details.

Everything was so clear. How could he not have noticed it? He must have been blind.

Now, for example, he saw

the way they looked at each other. Even in the kitchen, at the table, in the morning. The glances between her and the Nazi, glances of shared understanding, glances that spoke of shared memories and secrets. And he was sitting there at the table with them and didn't notice. What an idiot.

Now, for example, he saw

how he had embarrassed himself when he asked if he could go along to the movie. Their last night together: an Italian restaurant, a movie, and then her bed. And then he asks, what an idiot, if he could go along to the movie. As if it were the most natural thing in the world. She and Nazi must have roared with laughter once he left them alone in the apartment. And felt a little bit sorry for him since he was such an idiot.

Now, for example, he saw

how he met them outside the movie. "Ann-Ka has told me about you," Lotta had said. Yeah, right. And what had Ann-Ka the Duck said about him? Probably that she knew this super-persistent mega-idiot.

Now, for example, he saw

how it was at the movie, and how it was when they were on their way home from there. He actually thought that he was out with her. He thought that it was him and her. And then three others. That 2 + 3 = 5. He didn't see that it was two couples who were walking there. Two couples and him. 2 + 2 + 1 = 5. And he was the one. The extraneous and unwelcome and unwanted fifth wheel. And he didn't notice it. What a mega-mega-idiot.

The days went by.

He lay in his bed, he walked around like a zombie in his room, he never went outside, he didn't answer the phone and didn't open the apartment's outer door when the doorbell rang.

Summer vacation ran its course.

One night Mom came and sat on his bed.

"You," she said, seeming worried, "what's the matter? What's happened?"

He didn't answer.

"Won't you tell me?"

He lay there in silence.

"Is it love trouble?" Mom sighed. "Is it something with Ann-Katrin? You can always talk to me . . ."

He stared up at the ceiling.

"I might be able to help," she said, her voice serious, "because if there's anything I'm an expert in, it's love trouble. That's the only thing in life . . . the only thing I've been really good at, I think . . . at messing things up for myself . . ."

He looked at her in surprise but said nothing. She was talking to him almost as if he were a friend. As if he were a grownup.

". . . and at having children, of course," she continued and smiled. A soothing Mom smile. Now she was Mom again.

He shook his head and sighed weakly, and after a while she left the room.

Yes, the way Mom had talked to him surprised him. But as for whether she would be able to help him—no!

No one in the whole world could help him.

No one in the whole world.

Well, maybe one person.

But he didn't want to talk to her. He couldn't see her. He would never see her again.

Love trouble?

You don't understand anything, Mom.

This movie isn't about love, he thought later that night. It's about falling in love, about jealousy and longing and . . . and sex . . . and about a mega-idiot. But not about love. I don't know what love is, he thought.

Then Mom opened his door a crack and a narrow strip of light fell into the room.

"Are you asleep?" she whispered.

He shut his eyes and pretended to be asleep again.

Mom came into the room and walked over to his bed. She put her hand on his forehead. Her soft Mom hand.

"I love you," she whispered.

After a little while she left the room.

Ugh, he thought. Stupid Mom. You've watched too many Hollywood movies.

I love you I love you I love you I love you.

They say that all the time in movies.

They don't really mean anything when they say it.

No. I've never experienced love, he thought.

He had already decided that there was no point in living any longer.

There was no point to a life after Heart's Delight.

He had decided.

The only question was how.

A telephone

Now he has taken the light gray telephone from the book-shelf and placed it in front of him on the desk.

The phone is almost the only thing on the desk. Just a bottle of pills. A bottle of blue pills.

Everything else is gone now.

It has taken all evening, but now everything is gone.

He sits and stares at the silent telephone.

Life or death.

You have my fate in your hands, he thinks.

The phone sits silently.

I could call, he thinks after a little while. *I* could call.

No! The rules of the game have to be followed. No cheating. Not now.

But I could call just to find out if she came home, he thought. Maybe something happened.

But . . .

Yes, something might have happened. She might have been delayed. Maybe she's somewhere where there's no phone. She hasn't forgotten, it's not that she doesn't care, she just can't . . .

I can call to find out if she's home. Not talk to her. Just to find out if she's home.

He thinks and picks up the receiver.

Now I've really talked myself into it, he thinks and starts dialing her number. The first three numbers are easy. Then he hesitates.

Just 2564 away from her now.

He puts the receiver back.

He picks it up again.

Bzzzzzzzzzzzz.

Now he dials the first four numbers before he stops himself. He's just 564 away from her.

He hangs up with a sigh.

Third attempt then. Third and final attempt.

He collects himself, takes a deep breath, picks up the receiver and starts steadily and rhythmically dialing her phone number: first number—second number—third number—fourth number—fifth number—sixth number—

Stop. Dead stop.

She is only a 4 away. He is only one 4 away from her. Just a single lonely 4. Just . . .

No. No!

He presses the receiver back onto the phone. He presses hard. No. It would be wrong.

What's said is said.

What's thought is thought.

He sits at his desk and stares at his phone. It sits silently.

Ann-Katrin, the former Heart's Delight, gets in

"Can you watch Hanna tomorrow?" Mom asked one rainy Thursday at the beginning of August.

"Sure," he says, shrugging his shoulders.

"Then next week I have vacation," Mom continued. "We'll all do something together then. Go to Copenhagen! Go to Tivoli Gardens, the amusement park! We'll think of something. I'm sure Krister can take a few days off. And you have to get out of the house a little. And get some fresh air. You're as pale as a sheet."

"Hooray!" shouted Hanna and started jumping up and down. "Tivoli! Hooray! Can I get one of those giant waffle cones, Mom? Dipped in chocolate with sprinkles on top? Mom? Can I? And cotton candy, Mom?"

"Quit nagging," he said, irritated.

"Quiet, sheet face," Hanna said and started chanting: "Sheet face, sheet face, eat paste, sheet face . . ."

"Tomorrow we'll be alone, just you and me," he hissed.

"And then you're . . ." But he wasn't really threatening her. And he would buy her cotton candy at Tivoli. And she knew it.

It was that Friday when he was home alone with Hanna when the doorbell rang.

"Don't open it!" he quickly shouted as Hanna rushed toward the door.

"Why not?" she asked, stopping in her tracks.

"It . . . it might be a burglar," he said. "A mean burglar. A thief. A crook. A robber."

She stood still in the hallway. The doorbell rang again.

"Do you think it's a robber?" Hanna whispered.

He nodded seriously. "Mmm."

Then Hanna froze and pointed:

"The mail slot. He's opening the mail slot . . ."

"Hello! Are you home? Is anyone home?" a voice said through the mail slot.

A voice that he knew all too well. Hanna also recognized the voice and ran to the door before he could stop her.

"You're not a robber," she said happily and kneeled to look through the mail slot.

"No, I'm not a robber," the voice said. "I'm Ann-Katrin. Do you remember me, Hanna?"

Hanna nodded cheerfully.

"Mmm-hmm. You're the one who had the nice sandals. Who can't help it if you have red hair."

There was a laugh on the other side of the door.

"That's right. Hey, Hanna, is your big brother home?"

"Mmm-hmm," said Hanna. "He's babysitting me today."

"I want to talk to him," said Ann-Katrin. "Can you open the door, Hanna?"

"Sure," said Hanna.

And opened the door.

And so, at last, she gets in. The former Heart's Delight.

"Hi."

She stopped in the doorway of his room. He was sitting on his bed. He looked up for an instant but said nothing.

"Have you been sick?" she asked.

He didn't answer.

"You're so pale. You're completely white."

"Mom says that he's a sheet," Hanna said happily, appearing next to Ann-Katrin in the doorway. "But on Monday we're going to Tivoli and I'm going to get—"

"Hey, Hanna," Ann-Katrin said and took off her watch, "I want to talk to your brother for a bit. In peace and quiet. Keep your eyes on this watch. If you leave us alone until the big hand gets to the three there, then I'll go down to the Närköpet store and buy you the biggest ice cream they have."

"A jumbo cone?" Hanna asked, lighting up.

"A jumbo cone!"

"Then I'll do it!" Hanna said. "Until it's on the three."

She scampered off and Ann-Katrin came into the room. She pulled the desk chair over and sat right in front of him.

"You . . ." She looked at him carefully and seriously. "You . . . I'm missing a friend that I used to have."

He swallowed but said nothing.

"I tried calling you a hundred and eleven times. About. And I'm sure I've been here twenty times and rang the doorbell," she continued. "How should I get in touch with you?"

"Write a letter," he whispered without smiling.

She shook her head.

"I'm not that good at writing letters. Not like you. And I want to talk to you, and I think that—"

He interrupted her suddenly, his voice resolute:

"I want my letters back."

She looked up and shook her head.

"Not on my life. They aren't your letters. They're my letters. You sent them to me. And I have them in my dresser drawer with a red silk ribbon around them. All twelve of them. You won't get them back. Never."

Her answer satisfied him even though she said no.

The letters meant something to her. And when he was gone the letters would still be around, and she would read them and regret what she did and cry . . . Good!

"A penny for your thoughts," she tried.

He shook his head but didn't say anything.

"You . . . We have to talk," she said then. "Everything went so badly when you came home from America. I've thought about it a lot. And you don't seem like you're doing that well either, I can see that."

You're so tan and freckled and healthy, he thought bitterly. You don't look like you're suffering. And whose fault is it if I'm not doing well? Maybe I've come down with some disease? And what do you care?

He thought, but didn't say anything.

"You . . ." she started again, getting up from the chair. "It was a mistake, you . . ."

She walked over to the window.

Talk away, he thought. Just keep on talking.

"I . . ." she continued, "I've never met anyone . . . anyone who I felt like it was so easy to . . . to be with . . . as you. As with you. I felt like I could be myself when I was with you."

She had been standing with her back to him, but now she turned around and continued with a little laugh:

"I knew exactly what I wanted to say to you. I've been preparing this speech for several weeks, but . . . now the words escape me—couldn't you help me out a little? I want my friend back, I want—I want to keep getting to know you . . . you . . ."

A friend, he thought, yeah, that's what I've been, yeah. A buddy, a pal, an acquaintance, company on the bus, yeah. So she's in the habit of sleeping with her friends, then?

"It was a mistake," she said, kneeling down in front of him, "it was a mistake, and it was my fault, we should never have ended up . . . in your bed, I knew it was stupid, but—it was my fault . . . I couldn't resist you . . . you . . . were so adorable, you are so . . . so adorable, do you know that?"

He jumped up.

"What is it?" she said nervously. "What is it?"

"Bath . . . bathroom," he stammered. "Have to go to the bathroom."

And he rushed past her into the bathroom and locked the door. He stood there leaning over the sink.

I can't cry, he thought, breathing heavily. I cannot start crying.

For a long, long time he splashed cold water on his face, then he flushed and went back to his room.

She looked at him closely as he crawled back onto the bed.

"It's okay to cry," she said.

Adorable? he thought in the silence that followed. For her, adorable means the same as handsome. What she wanted was a mannequin.

He thought, but didn't cry.

"Mmm. I knew that it was a mistake," she continued after a couple of minutes, "and if I'd been able to talk to you then, afterwards, it wouldn't have had to be like this, but . . . but you left for America, and . . . then you came home and . . ."

And found Nazi-Hans in your bed, he thought.

"You don't need to be jealous of Hans-Peter," she said. "You never need to be jealous of anyone. I want you to be my friend—ugh, that sounds so stupid, but that's what I want. I want to keep you. Forever. But I'm not your Yoko Ono."

No, he thought, and once you've found your John Lennon you'll forget me, your good friend. What do you need me for then? What?

"It doesn't need to be like this," she said suddenly and got up anxiously, "it doesn't have to be either/or. It must be possible to be friends—fuck, won't you help me? Don't just sit there staring."

She looked angrily at him. But did she have tears in her eyes? There was something glistening there, he could see that before he lowered his gaze.

He remained silent.

"Don't you want to see me? Do you just want . . . want to forget me? Couldn't you just talk to me at least?"

No, he thought.

Yes, he thought.

No, he thought.

And said nothing.

"So sit there, then. Sit here and feel sorry for yourself. Because I'm not planning to . . ."

Why was she angry?

He swallowed and looked at his feet. That one sock is inside out, he thought.

"If you don't say something now, if you don't start talking to me, then I'm leaving," she said.

Do that, he thought, I've made up my mind. There's nothing you can say that . . .

No. No, don't go, he thought. Don't go! Stay! Save me . . .

Then Hanna opened the door.

"It's on the three now," she said expectantly.

No one in the room reacted.

"It's on the three now. The long hand. We're going to buy ice cream now, you promised. Come on!"

She stamped her foot in frustration, and Ann-Katrin turned to face her.

"Okay, I'm coming," she said with a sigh and a quick glance at him. "I'm coming now. That was a jumbo cone, right?"

He heard them out in the hall.

"Did you guys kiss?" Hanna asked, giggling.

"No . . ."

"Why not?"

"He doesn't want to."

"He's nuts," said Hanna.

And the front door banged shut.

Ten minutes later, Hanna and Ann-Katrin were back. They stood next to each other and looked at him, still sitting there on his bed. Hanna's face was already covered with ice cream.

"Yum," Hanna slurped. "Yummy."

"I'm leaving now," Ann-Katrin said.

He said nothing.

"I'm taking the night train to visit my dad. And go sailing with him. For two weeks. We're going to sail along the Höga coast. I'm coming home the Saturday before school starts."

He said nothing.

"Do you want me to call you then? Do you want me to call you when I get home?"

He said nothing.

"Of course he does," said Hanna. "Of course you want her to call, nutso. So say it. Say that you want her to."

But he said nothing.

And she turned around to leave.

Then:

"Yes . . ."

Just a hoarse whisper. But Ann-Katrin heard him and stopped. She turned to face him again.

"Yes, ahem, call. Call when you come home," he whispered.

She nodded seriously.

"Mmm. I'll call on Sunday, then. I'll probably get home late Saturday night."

"No," he whispered, shaking his head. "Call on Saturday. Call when you come home. Even if it's late. I'll be awake."

"Okay then." She nodded. "Then I'll be going. Bye, Hanna. Have a good time in Copenhagen. And take care of your big brother."

"Bye."

And she left.

Now I've placed my life in your hands, he thought.

I'll wait until the Saturday before school starts.
But if you don't call:
Hello, blue pills. Welcome.
Goodbye, Life.
Thank you and goodbye.

A packet of seeds

He happens to cast a glance at the floor and catches sight of the corner of a piece of yellow paper sticking out from under his desk. He bends down and picks up—a packet of seeds.

The packet of seeds, yes. He'd forgotten it. It was here on the desk earlier tonight. It was between the plant and "Uti Vår Hage." It probably blew down when he opened the window, he thinks. He looks at it:

NELSON BROTHERS SEED COMPANY
Tingsryd, Sweden
LEMON BALM

He turns the packet over and reads on the back side:

LEMON BALM
Melissa officinalis
PERENNIAL herb
Seeds for approximately: 50 plants
Sowing: Indoors in April–May for
transplant outdoors at the end of . . .

In May, yes. That was when he had bought this packet of seeds. It was after that that he had been to . . . her house. The first time. When she gave him the plant.

Then he had bought the seeds so that he could plant lemon balm himself and fill his whole windowsill with light green herbs and his whole room with the scent of lemon.

But the seeds had never made it into the dirt.

Without thinking about what he's doing, he tears the packet of seeds open and pours the tiny seeds into his right hand. Without thinking about what he's doing, he stuffs a few of the small black seeds into his mouth. And starts chewing.

The telephone, yes.

It sits there on the desk in front of him.

It sits silently.

Heart's Deli . . .

Now the movie is almost over.

Now the movie has caught up to him, the young man who is sitting there at his desk and thoughtfully chewing on some tiny seeds. How will the movie end?

He has seen many different endings to the movie. For example, he saw how Mom and the others come home from the cabin and find him at his desk, bent over his desk, and Mom thinks that he's sleeping, of course, and comes into the room to wake him up.

"Hello, we're home . . ." And just then she discovers the bottle with the blue pills next to him, and she understands that he's . . .

"IIIIIEEEEEEEEEEEEEEEHHHHHHH!!!"

Dead.

He has seen his mom crying desperately.

"Why? I don't understand. Why? What did I do wrong?"

He has seen his own funeral, how she stands there, Ann-Katrin, she stands a little to the side, she's as white as chalk and she holds three blood-red roses in her hand, and she knows, she knows all too well that it is for her sake. That it's her fault. He has seen how she can't live with the guilt, how she takes her own life also.

Yes, he has even seen how they meet again, in some kind of heaven.

Yes, now the movie will end soon. But how?

He chews on the small seeds, and something happens to him.

Right now, something happens to him. Does it have to do with the black seeds?

First he thought that they didn't taste like anything at all, that they were far too small to have any taste, but now he notices a faint, faint taste of . . . No, he doesn't know what it is, but the taste awakens a memory in him,

a memory of something a very long time ago,

a memory with sun in it,

a soothing memory.

He can't put it into words, and he doesn't see any images, it's only there as a feeling.

And something happens to him.

The large, heavy lump in his body was not made of concrete after all. It was made of ice. He sees that, now that his sunny memory got it to melt. And all the horrible rats are suddenly gone.

"Forgive me," he says to himself and walks with determined steps toward the bathroom, with the bottle of blue pills. He puts it back in the medicine cabinet, at the top in the back.

"Forgive me," he mumbles when he sits back down at his desk. I wasn't serious, he thinks. I never really meant it. It was just a feel-sorry-for-me-ploy.

But who is he apologizing to?

RIIIIING!!

The telephone. It does not sit silently any longer. Now it's ringing. And the sound makes him jump.

But he doesn't answer.

RIIIIING!!

He stares at the phone. He puts his hand on the receiver. But he doesn't pick up the receiver. He doesn't answer.

RIIIIING!!

He lays his cheek against his hand on the receiver. But he doesn't pick up the receiver. He doesn't answer.

RIIIIING!!

Now he's crying. The tears fall onto his hand, which is lying on the telephone receiver. But they aren't tears of desperation anymore. They are tears of release. And he doesn't pick up the receiver.

RIIIIING!!

"You . . . It's over now. It's finished now," he whispers without picking up the receiver. "You . . ."

RIIIIING!!

He cries, bent over the phone.

He cries happy tears.

But he doesn't answer.

RIIIIING!!

"You . . ."

He doesn't answer. He doesn't pick up the receiver.

RIIIIING!!

"You. You want to know something?" he whispers without picking up the receiver.

RIIIIING!!

"I love you."

The telephone falls silent.

The telephone sits silently.

First-person singular. And plural.

Him and him and him.

Who am I trying to fool? he thinks with tears in his eyes. I mean: *I* think with tears in my eyes.

It is, after all, about me.

Him is me. I am him.

First-person singular: I.

There is no movie anymore. There is no main character. It's over now.

But there is me.

And you. Somewhere out there, there's you.

And I'm glad there's you. And I'm glad that I know that there's you.

And somewhere, in a remote corner somewhere, there's a little we. A little we that will still be there no matter what happens now.

First-person plural: We.

I. And you.

We.

What you would have seen and heard (2)

Yes, if you for some reason had stood outside that building, and maybe inside stairwell A, on that Saturday evening in August, what would you have seen and heard?

Someone threw a pot from a balcony, yes. A pot with a lemon balm plant in it. Heart's delight. And a black Frisbee. Although actually it was a record. And a Swiss Army knife.

And the five balloons that lifted off were of course five inflated condoms.

And someone threw things into the garbage chute.

And someone went to the laundry room with a sheet.

And someone put a wrapped package with a curly ribbon outside a door on the third floor.

That is what you would have seen and heard.

That was all that happened. Really.

The rest was just a movie.

Well, actually, one more thing: At exactly one a.m. that night, a telephone rang in an apartment on the second floor. And if you snuck in and stood outside the door to that apartment and carefully opened the mail slot, you could have heard someone in the apartment say:

"I love you."

simon
pulse
fiction:

Edgy. Real.
Daring.

Friction
0-689-85385-8

Who's Your Daddy?
0-689-86440-X

Dead Girls Don't Write Letters
0-689-86624-0

Hanging on to Max
0-689-86268-7

The Long Night of Leo and Bree
0-689-86335-7

Color of Absence
0-689-85667-9

All That Remains
0-689-83442-X

Crying Rocks
0-689-85320-3

coming soon:

Beauty
0-689-86235-0

Seven Tears into the Sea
0-689-86442-6

Massive
1-4169-0207-4

Simon Pulse · Simon & Schuster · www.SimonSaysTEEN.com

As many as 1 in 3 Americans
who have HIV... don't know it.

TAKE CONTROL.
KNOW YOUR STATUS.
GET TESTED.

To learn more about HIV testing,
or get a free guide to HIV and
other sexually transmitted diseases:

www.knowhivaids.org
1-866-344-KNOW